I0675199

DESTRUCTIVE FATE

Destructive Series: Book Two

Abel Ozuna

AOIV Publishing

Dedication

This book took me almost five years to write (sorry to the readers of Book One, don't send hate mail, please! Ha ha). I just kept writing and erasing, thinking, this isn't good enough. I finally said, the heck with it and put it out. I guess every writer goes through this, right?

Well, since starting the book, I lost someone I love with my entire being. My baby sister, Jasmine. She was the light in any dark room, and her smile was the cure for everything bad. Although she was taken from us so young, she was a wise owl and lived a lot for someone who had just turned 21.

To "Shamin", my dear baby sister: I'll love you forever and ever. I can't wait until the day we are together again. I hope that you're dancing with the Angels and saving my spot up there. And most of all, I hope that I make you proud.

With Love,
"Gigi"

CONTENTS

PROLOGUE

Six months ago, I shattered the universe.

On every Fae's sixteenth birthday, they are to choose one of the two different types of Fae: the Light or the Dark. This has happened for as long as anyone can remember, until I decided to not choose a side.

I chose myself and was transported to Zion, a place in between Heaven and Earth. I've spent the last few months learning how to handle my powers with the help of the Original Light Fae, Camila.

Camila has been in Zion since the Fae War and escaped here after her husband killed off their family members. She's tired of hiding and I'm ready to make my mark on the world.

We're going back to Earth and I hope that my family and friends are ready for what's to come.

CHAPTER ONE

"Camila, are you sure I'm ready to go back? Maybe we should stay here for another month or two."

Camila looked at her reflection in a gold-trimmed mirror and pulled her long silky hair from her face. "Aria, you're more than ready. You need to get back to your family and friends. Violet and Sebastian have been making their rounds with the Dark Fae and I'm afraid they're going to overturn the Trebles at any moment."

"I can't let that happen. Grayson's family are the type of Fae we need to represent the Dark. They are progressive. They are nice."

She started to gracefully walk towards me. "I know that you care deeply about the Trebles; however, I need you to remember: at the end of the day, they're still Dark Fae. Dark Fae are not always bad, but the word Dark does allude to some darkness they all can have in their souls."

"I know, I just don't see how the Trebles can, though. They love each other. They are nothing like Violet or Sebastian."

"You have not known the Treble family very long. How do you think they became the Dark Royals?"

"Um, I don't know. I've never thought about that."

She smiled at me. "Let's just say that they weren't always in charge and they weren't exactly voted into office."

"Do you know how they became the Royal family, Camila?"

"I do; however, I don't think I should be the one to tell you that story. Why don't you go back to your world and have a talk with them? I am sure your family misses you."

I let out a long sigh. "Yeah, I guess you're right. Are you going to come back with me?"

"I have a few things to tidy up here, but I will be back there very soon. I am sure my estranged husband will be ecstatic to see me. What do you think?"

"Yeah, I am sure he's going to love that. I really can't wait to see how Violet reacts. You know, with her wanting to marry him and stuff?"

Camila walked back towards her mirror and laughed. "Oh, they have my blessing. I wish them the best. Aria, why don't you get your things ready. Let's get you home."

CHAPTER TWO

I opened my eyes and I was laying on a large bed that was not mine. I jumped up and started to look around. What the hell? Where am I? Am I still in Zion?

My mom walked into the large room with tears in her eyes. "Oh, my God! Aria, baby, you're awake! Thank all things that are holy! Liam, get up here!"

I embraced my mom and asked, "Mom, where am I? How did I get here?"

"Sh, sh, sh, baby. We can answer all of your questions in a bit. I'm just so happy that you are home."

"Home? This isn't our home. How long have I been here?"

My dad ran into the room, trying to catch his breath. "Aria? Are you alright? Do you need something to eat or drink?"

"I'm okay, thanks. Where are we? Mom, why did you say that I'm home? This isn't home!"

She looked at my dad and he answered for her. "Honey, you've been gone for six months. A lot has changed since your reckoning. This is just one of those things."

"Why didn't anyone mention this to me when I'd visit you all?"

My mom answered, "We didn't want you to feel like you had to cut your time with Camila short. We agreed that we'd wait for you to come back."

"So, where are we?"

"Liam, I'm going to call Alexia and the Trebles. They'll want to know Aria's back. Will you please fill your daughter in on what's going on?"

"Will you tell Grayson to come over? I need to see him."

She nodded her head and hugged my dad before she walked out of the room.

"Dad, I've missed you guys so much."

"I know, baby, we've missed you too. Your mom and I were going insane when you were taken to Zion. We had no idea what happened until we finally went to sleep the next night. Camila came to your mom and me and told us everything that had happened. She told me that she'd show you how to keep in touch with us and I'm glad she kept her promise."

"Yeah, she is really cool. I thought I died when I first got into Zion. It was all so beautiful."

"I'm happy that the Original Light Fae kept you under her wing. You couldn't have been in better hands after your reckoning. Now, back to the subject at hand. This is our new home. We are officially the Light Royal family. Lucas's body was never found."

"Are you serious? Is anyone still looking for him? Even if he was dead, wouldn't someone have found a body by now?"

"We are still searching for his body, but as you know, Sebastian Harper is back and he's not hiding anymore. He's been trying to take over the Trebles' reign. He has somehow manipulated some of their closest advisors."

"Wow, are all of the Trebles okay?"

Before my dad could answer, my mom walked back into the room. She walked over and stood next to my dad. "Grayson will be here soon and Alexia is on her way home. Declan is going to stay at his boarding school for now. It's not safe for him."

My dad looked at my mom with love in his eyes. I

asked him again, "Dad, are all of the Trebles okay?"

My mom answered me, "Yes, they're okay, for now."

CHAPTER THREE

"Mom, what do you mean that they're okay 'for now'? Are they okay or are they not?"

My dad answered me, "Aria, they're all alive if that's what you want to know. Apparently Grayson is coming over here and after he goes through security, he can fill you in on what's happening over at their home."

"Grayson has to go through security to talk to me? You've got to be kidding, Dad."

"No, I'm not kidding. I know you just got back but it's important that you remember you are the daughter of the Royal Light Fae family."

My eyes and body began to burn as I felt the different colors in them project off of the white walls. "I am your daughter, but it's important that each of you know, I didn't choose a side. I am both Light and Dark."

My mom shrieked. "Aria, calm down right now! You will not disobey your father and me in our home. We're doing you a favor here!"

"You're doing me a favor? Are you kidding me? You're doing your minor daughter a favor by allowing her to live under your roof?"

My dad shouted at me now, "Aria Whitelace! You know that is not what your mother meant. She meant we are doing you a favor, letting Grayson into our home. We have not even begun to discuss what you may or may not be!"

My body slowly cooled down and I started to put some tennis shoes on. "Well, I'm glad Grayson is coming over because I'm going to tell you all exactly what I am."

As if on cue, a man dressed in all white robes walked into my room. "Mr. and Mrs. Whitelace, your visitor from the Dark Royal family has been screened. He is in the grand hall whenever you're ready for him."

I mumbled, "The grand hall? Are you two serious right now?" I walked out of the room and followed the man down two large flights of stairs. When I walked into what I assumed was a library, I was stunned by the gold trim along the edges of the bookshelf. Man, this looks like Zion.

My mom's soft voice broke my thoughts. "It's beautiful, isn't it?"

"Ye-yeah. I was just thinking, it looks just like some of the rooms in Zion."

"Oh really?" Her eyebrows were raised now. "That's interesting. I wonder if Camila made Zion after living here."

"Camila used to live here? Are you kidding me?"

"I'm not kidding you. Rumor has it that the room you were in was once hers. As a matter of fact, that entire floor is named after her."

"Mom, are you telling me that I have an entire floor of this house to myself?"

"Well, not exactly. You have a couple of rooms, one for your clothes, another for your shoes. The other rooms are Alexia's."

"There's no way in hell we need this much room."

She laughed. "I know, but while we're here we may as well take advantage of it, don't you think?"

I nodded as my dad walked into the room. "Alright you two, let's get into the grand hall. Aria, I'm sure you're dying to see Grayson."

CHAPTER FOUR

As I followed my parents to the grand hall, my nerves started to get the best of me. *Aria, calm down, it's just Grayson. He's just as excited to see you as you are to see him. It's going to be okay.*

We stood in front of a pair of dark, wooden double doors and my dad signaled for me to walk in first. The large doors squeaked as I pushed them open. There he was.

Grayson Treble was standing a couple of feet in front of me and his eyes were lit up with anticipation. He gave me his perfect smirk as I ran towards him.

"Grayson, oh my God, I've missed you!"

"I know, I've missed you so much, too! I can't believe you're here. You're back!"

He leaned in and kissed me and I felt my skin spark off of his. He bit my lip as we ended our kiss. He looked at me with his violet eyes and I stared back at him with my differently shaded eyes.

"Aria Whitelace, I love you."

"I love you too, Grayson Treble."

My dad cleared his throat from behind us. "Alright, now that we've got our hellos out of the way, can we get to some business?"

I blushed. "Sorry, Mom, Dad. I, I just missed him so much."

My mom walked over and gave Grayson a hug. "It's okay, Aria. I know he's missed you too."

Grayson went on to shake my dad's hand and then let the bright glow of his eyes cool down. "Mr. and Mrs. Whitelace, thank you for inviting me into your home. It's quite nice."

I asked, "This is the first time you've been here?"

"Um, yeah. Your parents, being the Light Fae Royals, didn't really have to ask me here, Aria."

My mom added, "This is his first time in our home, but we have been meeting in a neutral zone quite often. Especially after Sebastian made it clear that he was serious about taking over his throne."

Grayson continued, "Aria, a lot has happened since you were taken."

"I can tell."

My dad interjected, "Grayson, why don't you tell Aria what's been happening with your family?"

"Okay, well, um, Sebastian and Violet have somehow infiltrated our home and have turned some of my family's most loyal supporters against us. I don't know what they're promising them, but it must be something good because our staff has reduced in half."

"Are you serious? Are they telling you why they're leaving?"

Grayson shifted around uncomfortably. "Not exactly. Most of them have tried to kill one of us. We're basically having to watch our own backs. My brothers and I have been sort of taking turns doing it."

"What about the Dark Fae guards? Are none of them around to help?"

"A few of them are, but most of them have gone to work for Sebastian. Another reason why I wanted to come today was to ask your family for help. Last night, my baby sister was taken from her school. Violet sent us a video this morning and she's got her."

I jumped up and felt the familiar burning sensation start to form behind my eyes. "Violet has Natalia? How did she get to her? Isn't her school protected by nothing but Royal guards?"

I looked at my parents. "Please tell me that it's not the same Fae school that Declan is at."

My mom's eyes started to tear up as my dad shouted, "Guards!"

A group of men ran into the room as one of them asked, "Yes, sir?"

My dad's jaw tightened. "Please go to the school of Fae. Get Declan home, now!"

CHAPTER FIVE

I cried out, "Declan's there? Are you kidding me? I thought he was going to a mundane school like I was?"

My mom answered me as my dad was on the phone with a council member. "We had to move Declan to the school of Fae when we became the official Royal Light Fae family. We didn't have a choice."

My sister, Alexia, walked into the room. "Aria, oh my God, I have missed you so much! You look so good!"

She was about to hug me but stopped when she saw my eyes were now fully lit with anger. She looked at my parents and then at Grayson.

"Grayson, what's going on in here? What's happened?"

"My sister was kidnapped from the Fae School!"

"That's not possible. That place is guarded with Dark and Light guards. Declan's there!"

I mumbled, "That's what I said."

Grayson put his hand on my arm to calm me down. "Aria, I'm sorry I've upset you. But I needed to come and tell your family. We need your help. Declan is there and it could have been him taken, but it wasn't. My family members are questioning the school's staff now and it's not going to be a happy ending for everyone there."

I asked, "What do you mean?"

"Well, my parents are going to be forced to punish the school's head of staff, and she is a Light."

My dad hung up his phone as he heard the last part of Grayson's sentence. "That's not going to happen. Not on my watch."

Grayson took his attention off of me and focused on my dad again. "I'm sorry, Mr. Whitelace, but my family is adamant that they're the ones who fulfill the punishment. If they do not, the other Dark Fae who remain loyal to us will question my family's motives."

"Grayson, you will not come into our home and tell me what your family thinks they're going to do with our Light Fae. I will meet with your family at the school first thing tomorrow. I will have a few of our council members with me and we will do our own investigation."

Grayson nodded his head. "I understand, sir. I will tell my parents that you will be there tomorrow. I don't know if our entire family will be there, though. We cannot leave our home unprotected."

My mom looked at my dad with worried eyes. "Liam, how could Violet have gotten past our guards?"

My dad stayed looking at Grayson but answered my mom. "I don't think she could have broken through the Light Fae portion of the school. She had to have gotten in from their side."

Grayson's eyes lit up. "Aria, I better get going. I will see you at the school tomorrow. I think you've got some more catching up to do with your family."

He leaned in to kiss me and the second our lips touched, that flaming desire sparked up again. This time, neither of us let that pull us away from each other.

My dad demanded, "That's enough. We'll see you tomorrow, Grayson."

Grayson slowly pulled away from me, eyes still lit, and then turned to smile at my dad. "Okay, see you tomorrow, Liam."

CHAPTER SIX

Alexia and I walked Grayson out of the house, and then she started to give me a tour of the entire building, starting on the fourth floor where my parent's room was. As she showed me my mom's private office, she asked, "Aria, what is Camila like?"

"Um, I don't know. She's kind of normal. I mean, she's like really pretty and super nice. I was telling Mom earlier that this house kind of resembles Zion."

"Really? Like, is she prettier than me?"

I laughed. "Well, let's just say on a scale of one to ten, you're a two and she's an eleven."

"Ouch! No need to be so harsh. Anyways, I really missed you, Aria."

"I missed all of you too. It was nice being able to talk with you all still, but it wasn't the same. I felt like we were on a video conference or something."

"Yeah, I know. It was really hard."

I started to fidget with some of my mom's books when I finally built up the courage to ask, "Alexia, what happened after my Reckoning?"

"Well, after you went full on psycho and threw that orb at the Blood Moon, your body like dissolved into thin air. We were all a little shocked and didn't know what to do."

"What did Violet and Ethan do?"

"They almost immediately took off. When we started talking with the Trebles we came to the conclusion that somehow, some way, you were going to be with Camila. We stuck around there until the next morning and when you didn't return, we went home and then that's when Camila contacted Mom and Dad. I'm a bit annoyed I wasn't able to see her."

"Well, that's all going to change soon. I don't know when, but it's going to happen pretty soon."

Alexia's voice was raised an octave out of excitement, "Are you serious? What do you mean? Are you saying she's coming here?"

"Um, yeah. She was going to come back with me but she said she had some things to take care of first."

"I can't believe she's coming back! Do Mom and

Dad know?"

I shook my head. "Nah, I haven't told them. Now, with the whole Fae school thing, I don't know if I'll get the chance to tell them."

My sister's face beamed. "I can't wait to meet Camila. I wonder how our dear aunt Violet is going to handle that news. I mean, you know Sebastian and Camila are still technically married."

I laughed. "Yeah, I don't know how Violet is going to react, but I hope that we are around when she finds out."

We walked out of the office and headed back down to our floor of our new home. Alexia started to tease me. "Aria, I'm really happy that you're back but please don't think that you can just go into my closet and take whatever you want out of it. I'll literally kill you."

I let my eyes glow for the dramatic effect. "I don't know that you could kill me even if you tried."

Alexia's blue eyes matched my glow and she was about to push me when a blinding light flooded the long hallway and we both fell to the ground.

My sister and I tried to regain our focus and then I saw her. Camila Harper, the Original Light Fae, was standing a few feet in front of us.

Her perfect teeth gleamed through her smile. "Hello, Aria."

CHAPTER SEVEN

I slowly stood back up and waved. "Hey, Camila. I guess, welcome home?"

Camila's soft laughter filled the room. "It's been a long time since I've called this place home." She looked around and peeked into my bedroom. "Aria, do you know that this was once my room?"

I nodded and saw Alexia's jaw drop. My sister mumbled, "Are you kidding me? You got her room?"

Camila walked closer to us and wrapped her arms around me. "Your parents have done a nice job here. It looks beautiful. I guess you can tell why I decorated Zion the way I did. It reminded me of this place. It reminded me of home."

She looked at my sister and then reached her hand out. "Hello, Alexia. My name is Camila Harper. From your reaction, I assume you know a little about me?"

Alexia's hand was shaken. "Ye-yes, ma'am. It's

such an honor to meet you. You have been missed."

Camila smiled and then walked a little past us, towards the stairs. Her walk was so smooth, it almost looked like she was floating. "I am going to find a guest room. I hear that we have to go to the school for the Fae children tomorrow. I would love to join your family."

My sister asked, "Would you like to have my room for the night? Aria and I can share a room."

"Why thank you, Alexia. That is so nice of you. May I ask that you two not bother your parents with my presence tonight? I'd like to surprise them in the morning."

Alexia looked at me as I answered Camila. "Yeah, sure, no problem. See you in the morning."

My sister and I got into my room and she immediately started to ramble. "Oh my God, Aria. Camila freaking Harper is here. She's in our house! Oh my God, why didn't you offer your room? She said this was her room at one point. Don't you think she was trying to give you a hint?"

"Alexia, calm down. Camila doesn't really expect anyone to read between the lines. She is a straight shooter. If she wanted my room she would have asked for it. She's selfless, she wants everyone around her to be comfortable before she worries about her comfort."

My sister sat on my bed. "Do you think Mom and Dad are going to lose their freaking minds in the morning? What if they walk into my room looking for me, but run into Camila? I want to see their faces when Camila just magically appears at breakfast."

"Yeah, I imagine that their faces are going to pretty much resemble yours. You should have seen yourself."

"Dude, do not even start with me. Her entrance was so godly. I wish when I walked into a room a blinding light appeared. I mean, isn't personal lighting every girl's dream?"

"I don't think that's every girl's dream. I think it's just yours. Now can you freaking get off my bed so I can go to sleep? You're sleeping on the floor."

CHAPTER EIGHT

The next morning Alexia and I were the first two people dressed and at the kitchen table. My mom and dad walked in together, both of them followed by their new assistants. My mom looked up at us and then looked at my dad.

"Um, Liam, am I seeing things? Are these our daughters?"

"Honey, I don't think you're seeing things. It's them alright."

My dad took his coat off and handed it to his assistant while he sat at the head of the table. "What do you two want? What are you up to?"

We looked at each other and laughed. I asked, "Why do we have to want something? We're just anxious to get to the school of the Fae."

My dad looked at my mom as she sat on the opposite end of the large marble table. Four servers walked into the room and set a plate of food in front of each of us. I was about to start eating when

I heard Camila's voice.

"Good morning, everyone."

My mom's face went pale as my dad spit out his coffee. He shuffled some napkins around and stood up. "Camila, my goodness, welcome home. Why don't you take my seat?"

Camila walked gracefully across the room as she smiled at us. "Thank you, Liam. No need, this was my home a long, long time ago. It is your family's now. You sit at the head of the table. I'll sit across from the girls."

My mom stood up. "Camila, would you like something to eat? The house chef makes the best breakfast."

"Thank you, Adalyn. I'll just have some fruit. I'm not much of a breakfast person."

Alexia leaned in and whispered, "Dude, no wonder she's so hot. Look at her plate compared to mine. I'm such a pig."

I laughed out loud and both of my parents glared at me. Camila broke the tension. "When will we be going to the school of the Fae? I hear that there's a Dark Royal Fae that's been taken from there?"

My dad answered her, "The cars are waiting for us. We're going as soon as we are through with breakfast. We're meeting the Dark Royals there. I don't know how much you know, but the Dark Royals want to be in charge of punishing the school's leader, who happens to be a Light Fae."

Camila murmured, "That's quite interesting. Do the Dark Royals not know the Fae Laws? We punish our own. Their punishments are usually far too harsh and often do not match the crimes."

My dad continued, "Well, yeah, they know the laws, but I think they are trying to challenge them. They're in a tough spot right now with Sebastian trying to take back his throne."

"My husband is so ambitious. It's quite obnoxious, to be honest. I cannot wait until we are reunited. He's not going to believe the things I know. The whole time he tricked his own kind into believing he was gone, he was hiding right under their nose. I saw it all and he has no idea."

My dad's assistant walked up and whispered into his ear. My dad stood up and said, "I think it's time for us to go. If you all would like, get your food to go. The Dark Royals are on their way to the school."

CHAPTER NINE

As we pulled into the parking lot for the large Fae school, Camila mumbled, "My goodness, it's been an eternity since I've been here. Do you all know that my family founded the school? I was part of the first Fae class. Oh, how time has flown by."

Alexia asked, "Are any of the Fae that you went to school with still around?"

"Um, I don't think so. But the Light Fae in charge of the school is the great-granddaughter to my best friend. I don't know that she knows that, though."

I stepped out of the car and then turned around to ask Camila, "Do you think anyone here is going to recognize you right away?"

"Oh, I think everyone is going to know who I am."

We walked towards the large, aged school and then I heard Grayson call my name from behind.

"Aria? Wait up!"

I turned around and his eyes lit up with excitement as we made eye contact. He picked up his walk to a jog and then was standing in front of me.

"Hey babe, how was your night?"

"Hey. Um, it was interesting."

"Oh really? What was so interesting about it?"

I smiled at him and then pointed towards Camila who was being greeted by the entire school's staff. Grayson asked, "Is that Camila Harper?"

I nodded. "Yup, it sure is."

"When did she come back?"

"She came back late last night, right before Alexia and I went to bed."

"Wow, that's crazy. I can't believe that both of the Original Fae are back."

"Yeah, I know. So, what did your parents say about your conversation with my parents?"

He smirked at me and said, "Well, I sort of sugar-coated it."

"Grayson, what do you mean, you sugarcoated it? My parents were pretty clear. They want to be the ones to punish the Light Fae, if they need to."

"Well, I didn't really tell my parents about the entire conversation. It's going to be quite interesting now that Camila is here though. Don't you think?"

"What do you mean?"

"Your parents are the Light Royals, but Camila is Camila Harper. She's the Original Light Fae. Without her and Sebastian, none of us would exist."

"I didn't think of that. But I'm sure Camila is going to be okay with whatever my parents decide."

"Alright, well, I guess we'll see. Aria, can you promise me something before we go inside, though?"

"Maybe, what do you want me to promise?"

"I need you to promise me that you'll stay out of the argument. You have to remember you are neither Light nor Dark."

"I can't promise that I'll stay quiet, Grayson."

He looked into my eyes. "Aria, please? My parents are pretty stressed out about everything going on right now and I don't want to give them a reason to not like you."

"I understand that, but I am not going to shut up just so someone can like me."

Grayson was about to protest when Camila

shouted, "Aria, are you coming inside with us?"

"Yeah, I'll be right there!"

I looked back at Grayson. "Let's go in there and get this over with."

CHAPTER TEN

Grayson and I walked inside of the large building and caught up with Camila and my family. I whispered to him, "Where is your family?"

"They're already in the conference room with the school's leaders. They're all waiting for us."

A short, stocky man with glasses began to lead our group up some stairs and then down a large hallway that was lined with portraits from top Dark and Light Fae Royals.

Grayson mumbled, "There's Sebastian's pathetic photo on the left."

"Yeah, and they have Camila's right in front of him. Talk about awkward."

Camila must have seen the photos because she asked the man, "Who do I have to talk to about the arrangement of these photos?"

The man stuttered, "Uh, um, you can speak with the head of the school. She's with the Dark Royals now."

"Thank you, kind sir." Camila showed off her perfect smile.

He immediately blushed. "Okay, the conference room is just through those doors. If any of you need anything, please feel free to ask the attendant standing in the room. They'll get you anything you need."

My parents thanked the man and then we all walked into the conference room. The room was a bit underwhelming compared to the grand rooms I've been in lately.

Alexia whispered, "This place looks so normal."

"Isn't it wonderful? Sometimes normal is a good thing, girls." Camila added.

My sister's face turned red from embarrassment. She walked to the back of the room, ignoring Mr. and Mrs. Treble. Cherise, Grayson's mom, shook everyone's hand and then offered me a hug. Braden, his dad, followed suit.

Cherise spoke first, "Camila Harper, what a lovely surprise. I was not aware that you would be joining us today?"

"No one really knew I was coming today. It was a bit of a surprise for everyone. I love surprises. Now, will someone please tell me what we are doing here today?" Camila said as she sat down across the table.

Braden responded, "As you may or may not know, our daughter was taken from this school yesterday and we want answers."

My dad asked, "Why haven't you asked the Dark guards that are assigned here? Surely, your daughter wasn't left unattended."

Braden's eyes lit up violet with anger. "We have asked all of the Dark guards that remain here. None of them were able to provide us with a sufficient answer."

Camila questioned him, "So then why are we here, with the Light Fae in charge of this school? Although she is a Light, she has taken an oath to protect and serve all the children at this school equally. Their family backgrounds, Light or Dark, do not affect the leadership of this school."

Cherise pushed back, "We understand that; however, we want to know how the leaders of this school were able to allow a child to just go missing. And not any child, but a child of the Dark Royal family."

Camila's eyes glowed and I was in awe. Her eyes glowed a bright blue that was mixed with a trim of gold. "If you understand the laws, then your family also knows that if the leader of this school broke his or her oath, they would immediately perish."

Before anyone could respond, the doors to the conference room flew open. My cousin, Ethan, and his mom, Violet, made their way into the crowded room.

CHAPTER ELEVEN

Violet's laughter sent chills down my spine. My eyes were glowing brightly and I felt my skin immediately start to burn. I looked down and saw that my skin had changed to speckles of different colors.

My estranged aunt looked at me with her violet eyes. "Aria, my dear, welcome home. How was your time in that horrid place?" She looked at Camila now. "What do you call it? Zeon? Zion?"

"You know exactly what my home is called. It is Zion. How dare you barge into the school of Fae like this! This is a sacred place!" Camila's body was now radiating with a bright golden light.

Ethan spat on the ground. "This place isn't sacred. It's a joke."

Camila raised her hands and Ethan's body was lifted into the air. "You have no idea who you're talking to, kid." He started choking and grabbing onto his neck as if he were trying to fight someone off of him.

Violet's hair started to swirl around as she lifted her own hands. A dark light surrounded Camila and she was starting to bend at the knee. I felt a warm pulse in my palm and then threw an invisible orb at my aunt.

"Get out of here!" I closed my eyes and shouted at her.

I continued throwing the orbs as one finally hit Violet and forced her out of the room. Camila kept her invisible grip around Ethan's neck as he started to turn purple in the face. "You are lucky I do not wish to spill Fae blood on these sacred grounds," she mumbled.

She dropped him and the Light guards immediately surrounded him. My dad shouted, "Take him to our prison! I want every guard we have there watching his cell."

One of the guards responded, "Yes sir. Are you sure we shouldn't take him to the Dark Fae prison?"

My dad looked at the Trebles and then said, "No, take him to ours. The Dark guards cannot be trusted."

Ethan tried to fight off the guards as they dragged him out of the room, but they overpowered him.

Alexia walked over to me. "How did they get into the school? The school has so many defensive protections around it."

"I don't know, but I do know I just pissed our aunt off even more."

She laughed. "Yeah, you did. She was not expecting you to have that kind of power."

Camila chimed in, "That's what Violet gets. No one should ever underestimate their enemy. When you underestimate someone or get comfortable, you lose any advantages you may have had."

"You have no right to hold a Dark Fae prisoner in your jails. They're a joke, Ethan will easily break out of them!" Mr. Treble exclaimed.

My dad defended himself. "How would you know what our security is like? Before you point fingers and say my guards are a joke, look at the situation we're in now. Your daughter is missing because of your incompetent and disloyal guards. And should I remind you that Ethan infiltrated your home not too long ago?"

Cherise spoke for her husband. "Mr. Whitelace, you are walking a fine line. Please, watch what you say."

"Mrs. Treble, I suggest you and your family leave this school, immediately." Camila warned Cherise.

Her eyes were glowing their magnificent gold. Grayson's dad agreed. "I think you're right Camila. We are leaving but know that we will soon be calling on all of our Dark Fae to remove their children from this building."

Camila held her hands out to show Mr. and Mrs. Treble the door. "That is your prerogative. I warn you though, you already have one Original Fae on your bad side. You do not want two. Remember, this is the safest place for all underage Fae."

CHAPTER TWELVE

Grayson walked his parents out of the room and then came back to try and calm my parents down. "Mr. and Mrs. Whitelace, I'm so sorry about all of this. I think my parents are just freaking out a bit. I think they need to just let everything soak in." He grabbed my hand and the sparking sensation sent shivers through my entire body.

"Grayson, I understand your parents are under a tremendous amount of pressure, but I am here to help. I left my safe haven to help all Fae. Yes, I'm a Light, but I believe in peace and harmony. War between the two of us isn't good for anyone." Camila answered before either of my parents could.

"That was intense. Grayson, your parents are pretty pissed but they left here without any real answers as to what happened to your sister. What do you think they're going to accomplish by pulling out all of the Dark Fae kids?" Alexia questioned him as she walked to my parents' side.

"I-I don't know, Alexia. I know that they mean well and I mean, for God's sake, my sister is missing."

Camila's golden aura was surrounding her body as she calmly spoke. "Grayson, no one is questioning the reason your parents are upset. I am, however, questioning their decisions. I think as the Royal family they would be more understanding and open to suggestions. Aria tells me your family is very progressive, hence the reason you two can still date. Do you think they would be open to meeting me on their terms? Maybe I can go to your family's home and speak with them again."

"Maybe it's worth a try. I can talk to them when I get back home." Grayson grabbed my hand and the normal burning sensation broke through his sweaty palms.

Camila's eyes widened. "You two are something special, just be wary of the Destructive Fire. Grayson, please, get your parents to talk to me again. I think that pulling all of the Dark Fae children from this school is exactly what Sebastian wants."

I was about to ask Camila about the Destructive Fire when my dad walked across the room and sat on a dark gray sofa. "Camila, that's interesting. Why do you think Sebastian would want the Dark Fae out of the school?"

Grayson answered before Camila could. "Sebastian wants us all to be divided. If we were all united against him and Violet, there's no way they would be strong enough to take us on. But if we are divided, he can use his loyal Dark Fae families to help fight off the Light Fae."

"Grayson's correct. I think that my estranged husband and Violet want to use the help of the Dark Fae to eliminate the Light. But I also think that once they've completed that, they will, together, turn on everyone who will not bow down to them. Sebastian wants total control of the Fae world, not partial. He wants to live among mundanes and be the superior species."

My sister, Alexia, whispered, "Would that be so bad?"

"Alexia, what was that?" my mom shouted.

"I mean, would it be so bad for us to be our true selves in front of the mundanes? Why are we forced to live in hiding?" Alexia was now red-faced with embarrassment.

"Mrs. Whitelace, it is okay. It's normal for young Fae to question things." Camila waved her hand at my mom to calm her down.

"Alexia, we can be our true selves, but we cannot let mundanes know what we are capable of. Their minds struggle with anything different. They will try and use us to benefit them and if any one of us were to deny helping them, they would turn us all into villains. We would be hunted down like the Fae in the 1600s. You may have learned about this in your schooling?"

"Are you talking about the Salem Witch Trials?" Grayson asked.

"Yes, that's right. The Salem Witch Trials. In 1692, mundanes found a group of Fae that were practicing with their infinities. Many of the Fae got away, but we lost 20 of our kind because the mundanes claimed they were dealing with dark magic." Camila's golden eyes were now dimmed with sadness as she continued to speak.

"Sebastian and I lost many relatives in those trials, so I understand why he wants his payback, but two wrongs do not make a right."

"Camila, I am so sorry. I had no idea that the witch trials were actually Fae trials." My mom's eyes were filled with tears.

"It's okay, it was a long time ago. But yes, they were all Fae. Witches wouldn't be caught alive by mundanes. They have the ability to disappear into thin air."

"Witches are real?" I asked.

"Yes dear, they are. Although many of them are in hiding. Even from us, the Fae." Camila turned her attention to Grayson again.

"Grayson, it's very important that your parents don't fall for Sebastian's trap. Please, stress the importance of our meeting to them."

"I understand. I will talk to them right away."

He smiled at her and then turned to kiss me. When our lips touched, the burning spark ran through my entire body and I felt the blues and purples radiating off of my skin. "I'll call you as soon as I get home, Aria. If you hear anything about my sister, please let me know."

I nodded as he walked out of the room.

CHAPTER THIRTEEN

We left the school and headed back to our house. When we pulled up to the mansion, I was taken aback by the beauty of our new home.

"Um, this is going to take some time to get used to."

"Yeah, I know, it's totally great though. I got used to it fairly quick. I mean, I can ask for a milkshake at any time of the day and someone gets it for me. And I don't have to make my own bed. It's great," Alexia teased as she was texting someone on her phone.

I got out of the vehicle and was greeted by a tall, dark-skinned man. "Ms. Whitelace, I am Hunter Spark. I have been assigned to your side."

"Um, hi Hunter. Please don't call me Ms. Whitelace, my name's Aria, and what do you mean you've been assigned to my side?"

Hunter looked at my parents, and my dad walked around the car to join Hunter and me. "Aria, you know that we're the Royal family, right?"

"Yeah, so why is Hunter my personal bodyguard? It's a little extreme. I'm pretty sure I can handle myself."

"Well, I'm sure you can, sweetie. But think of Hunter as someone who will always have your back."

"Yeah, Aria, think of me as a mere formality," Hunter smiled and then winked at me.

Alexia walked from behind the car and whispered, "Dude, your security guard is totally hot. Mine is an old man. I hate you."

I hit her on the arm as I felt my face begin to turn red. I ran my hand through my hair and walked towards the house with Hunter a couple of feet behind me.

We got into the house and my parents were talking to whom I assumed were their security guards when my dad's phone rang.

"This is Liam, go ahead." My dad put his finger on his mouth to hush the others in the room.

"Are you sure that it's her?" His face went pale now

as he stared at me.

"Have you all contacted the Trebles? ... Hmm, okay. Well, we will head over there soon."

My dad hung up the phone and then looked at my mom with saddened eyes.

"What is it, Liam? Who was that? What is going on?" my mom asked.

"It was the head of the Fae school. The Treble girl was found dead in their basement just now."

Camila's eyes widened with fury as she walked towards my parents.

"Liam, are you sure she's dead? Was she killed in the school? If so, that was an act of war. The school is sacred ground."

"They're still investigating the scene. They are waiting for the Trebles to arrive at the morgue to identify the body. Braden Treble is asking that we meet his family there."

"Oh Liam, that is horrible. Do you think Violet had something to do with it?" my mom cried out.

"I don't know, Adalyn. But if she did, she's going to regret it."

"You've got that right, and so will Sebastian,"

Camila added.

CHAPTER FOURTEEN

My family, Camila, and I rushed to the local Fae morgue. As we pulled up to a dark and gloomy building, Alexia sighed.

"There's no way this is the morgue. I mean, death is sad and all, but this doesn't look like it's even a building."

"The building is hidden under a Fae ward. We have to present ourselves to the guards to be allowed into the actual morgue. They do this so mundanes are not able to walk into Fae funerals," Camila said.

We all walked up to the two guards who were standing in front of a pair of rusted gates.

"This is the Light Fae Royal family. We are asking for entrance into the morgue," Hunter spoke for the group.

"Very well then, your entrance is granted." One of

the guards stared at us, his eyes glowing a deep purple.

The guards stepped aside, and the rusted gates made a loud screeching sound as they slowly opened.

"Okay, everyone, let's get in. I need to examine the body to see if Sebastian had something to do with this." We all stood still in awe of the beautiful building as Camila pushed forward.

"Aria, I've seen some cool stuff, but this funeral home is like *really* cool," Alexia whispered as we stared at the building. It was made of a gleaming crystal-like material.

"Girls, be respectful. The Trebles are in mourning right now. Let's not talk about how pretty the building is," my mom lectured us.

My sister and I lowered our heads and followed our parents into the large crystal building. As we were let into the waiting room, Hunter pulled me aside.

"Aria, would you like me to wait outside for you, or shall I wait here?"

"I don't know, whatever you want to do is okay. And just so we are clear, you don't have to be so formal with me. My parents are the Light Royals, but I'm just me. I'm just Aria."

"Okay, sounds good. I'll wait here then. I don't want to leave you alone." He smiled at me and showed off the most perfect set of teeth I have ever seen.

"Uh, um, ok-okay," I stuttered and tried to walk away but when I turned around, I saw Grayson. His jaw was shut tight and tears were running down his sculpted jawbone.

"Grayson, oh my God. I'm so sorry about your sister. Are you okay?" I walked closer to him and then put my arms around him.

"How do you think I'm doing? My sister was just found dead." He pushed me away and I saw his eyes turn to a bright violet color.

"Who's that?" He was pointing to Hunter.

"Um, that's my bodyguard." I felt tears starting to build up as I looked at Grayson and the pain he was in.

"He's a bit young to be your bodyguard, don't you think?"

"Uh, I don't know, Grayson. Why are we talking about Hunter? He's just a guard. You have them too. Have you found out anything about what happened to your sister?" I tried to hug him again.

"My guards don't look like that. And no, we haven't." He pulled away from me again as Camila walked up to us.

"Grayson, I'm so sorry for your family's loss. Are your parents here? I really need to see them."

"They're in there with the mortician and the Fae's school guards." He pointed towards the back of the room at a set of doors.

"Thank you, I am going to find out who did this to your sister. And believe me, they're going to pay for this. No one attacks a child, Light or Dark, on sacred grounds." Camila's eyes were golden again.

"Camila, if Sebastian did this, I need to be the one to kill him."

"We will cross that bridge when we get there." Camila gave him a half-smile as she walked towards the other room.

"Grayson, I need you to promise me you won't do anything stupid. You know if Sebastian did it, you won't be able to kill him on your own. He's an Original."

"You're right, maybe I can ask your hunky guard for help." He pointed at Hunter and this time, Hunter saw him. Hunter's eyes lit up blue as he walked towards us.

"Aria, is there a problem?" Hunter spoke to me, ignoring Grayson.

"No, I'm fine. You can wait outside now, Hunter."

I felt the heat from his body next to me as he stared at Grayson. "Alright, but I'll be right outside if you need me."

Grayson was about to say something I'm sure he'd regret, when we heard a woman's loud screeching cry from the room Camila had just entered.

CHAPTER FIFTEEN

Grayson, Hunter, and I rushed behind my parents and Alexia into the viewing room.

"I can't believe that's my baby! My baby!" Cherise was crying and being held up by two of her guards.

"Mrs. Treble, I am so sorry for your loss. We will find out who is responsible for this." Camila's voice was soft and soothing.

"I already have my oldest boys looking into this. The Fae school was supposed to be guarded. How did this happen?" Braden, Grayson's dad, asked in tears.

"Mr. Treble, everyone knows that the Fae school for the Light and Dark children is a sacred ground. There is only one person that I can think of that would be stupid enough to do something like this. And there's only one person with the power to get into that school."

"Are you talking about Sebastian Harper?" my dad asked with a shaky voice.

"I am. I am sure he had something to do with this. I can't be the only one who finds it strange that after your daughter goes missing, Violet and Ethan Whitelace, show up at the school?" Camila answered.

"Camila, should we shut down the school until further notice? I don't think that it's safe for everyone's children to stay there. Even with the guards, if Sebastian wants to get into the school, he can," my mom said.

"No, I don't think that's the right thing to do. Later, I will go by the school and I will be staying there until further notice. The protection of everyone's children, Light and Dark, is my priority. They are our future and how we respond to this is critical." Camila started to walk closer to the sheet-covered body of Grayson's sister.

"Do I have your family's permission to view the body? I need to see if there are any clues as to what happened. I may be able to look through her eyes and see exactly what happened."

"Yes, please do!" Mrs. Grayson cried out.

"Would you all really like to be present for this?" Camila asked.

Everyone stared at each other for a couple of seconds when Mr. Treble finally responded, "I trust that everyone here wants to find out who is responsible for this and that whatever you find will be kept in this room."

"Very well then, if someone could get me a step ladder so I can be above the body." We stayed quiet as Hunter got Camila the step ladder from across the room. He opened it up and she slowly stepped on it.

"Everyone, please remember that I'm going to try and see through the child's eyes. Whatever I say or see will be through her. Please, remain silent. If you cannot do that I ask that you leave the room."

No one moved, and she nodded as she lifted her hands and let her golden aura surround the small lifeless body.

CHAPTER SIXTEEN

Camila's hands were shaking with the bright golden light I've grown accustomed to seeing her use. Suddenly, the lights in the room began to flicker.

"Aria, do you think she's gonna be able to see through her eyes?" my sister whispered to me as the lights in the room completely turned off and we were sitting in darkness.

I glanced around the room and saw blue and purple eyes suddenly light up. The table that the youngest Treble was laying on suddenly began to shake violently.

"My dearest child, show me your murderer. Show me, the Original Fae, what happened to you!" Camila's body was now floating in the air.

"Please, please don't do this! My parents are the Dark Royals. We are a Dark family!" Camila was shouting out, but the voice we all heard belonged to Grayson's sister.

Camila's body suddenly fell to the floor, next to the table, and the lights slowly turned back on.

Hunter ran to help Camila up from the ground.

"Thank you, I'm okay. I just need to sit down for a minute." She leaned on him as he helped her walk to a chair.

"Wh-What did you see? Who did this to our baby?" Cherise Treble began to scream through her tears.

"Mrs. Treble, although I did not see Sebastian Harper, I did see who took your daughter's life." Camila looked at my family with a grim face.

"Well, spit it out! Who did it?" Mr. Treble was shaking with fury.

"It was Violet and her son, Ethan." Camila's face looked weak for the first time since I've met her.

"How did they get past her guards?" my mom shrieked out as my dad asked Camila what we were all thinking.

"I am going to find out as soon as I can get some of my energy back. I have only seen into someone's death a few times, and it takes a tremendous amount of energy. But I can tell you that Ethan was the one who delivered the final blow. He was the last person she saw."

"Are you sure it was Ethan?" Grayson asked. His eyes were now lit an extremely bright purple.

"Yes, Violet was taunting him. She was holding the child down as she told her son to prove his loyalty. He used some dark powers to take the life from her."

"I am going to kill him! I have to kill him!" Grayson started rushing out of the room in anger when the Dark Fae guards chased after him and held him down.

"You will not do such a thing, Grayson! We will find them and we will make them pay, but it's too dangerous for you to go now. I will not lose another member of this family!" Mr. Treble was shouting now.

"Camila, let's get back to the school. My wife will stay here, as our eldest sons are on their way back here now." Braden kissed his wife on the cheek as we all started walking towards the door.

"Camila, promise me, you will make sure the other kids are safe. We cannot let this happen to another family," Cherise pleaded.

"I promise I will do everything I can to make sure this does not happen again."

CHAPTER
SEVENTEEN

We rode to the Fae school in an awkward silence until my sister spoke.

"Aria, what was Grayson so mad about? What were you two talking about?"

"I don't think it's really any of your business, Alexia. And maybe he was mad because he just found out our cousin and aunt killed his sister?" I threw a piece of gum at her when the Fae school's guards opened our doors.

My sister and I stepped out of the car and followed my parents to the front of the school, where I saw Camila standing with the head of the school.

"Aria, would you like something to eat? You haven't eaten today, and I need to you keep your energy up." Hunter was smiling at me and I felt my knees shake with excitement.

"Um, sure, any kind of soup will be fine. I'm not

too hungry." I looked at my sister, who was looking at me suspiciously.

"Uh, Alexia, do you want anything to eat? Hunter is going to get me some soup."

"Yeah, I'll have a tomato soup. Thank you, Hunter." Hunter bowed his head at my sister and me and then walked off.

"Aria, he totally likes you. None of us have really eaten today, and none of our guards asked if we wanted food."

"Shut up, Alexia! He just wants me to stay energized, that's all." I felt myself blush as I lied to my sister.

"Uh-huh. Are you sure that Hunter has nothing to do with Grayson's bad mood?"

"I-I don't know. Grayson's just really not himself right now. Can we quit with the twenty questions now?"

We walked towards Camila and she greeted us with a warm and soothing smile.

"Hello, girls. I see your parents already made their way into the school. I understand they have meetings to attend. Would you like to join me and Grayson in the basement? We're going to review the crime scene."

"Grayson's here already?" I asked.

"Yes, he is. He was going to ride with his father and me, but he ended up driving on his own. He said he needed some time to cool off."

"I see. Um, yeah, we'll go with you."

As we followed Camila through the school, Alexia and I stared at the school's surprising guard presence. There was a guard standing outside of every classroom and restroom.

"Dude, they've already stepped up their security like crazy. Do you think they're all Light guards?" Alexia asked.

"I don't think so. I think it's a mix but mainly Light. I think the Dark Fae have some leaks they're working through."

We walked down a long stretch of stairs and saw that every guard that greeted us was indeed a Light Fae.

"Camila, are there any Dark guards left here?" I asked as she opened the door to the basement floor.

"There are about ten Dark Fae guards left here, and they have been personally vetted by the Dark Royal Family. Until they know who they can trust, we've all agreed it's best if the Light Fae guards took over."

I entered the basement while Camila closed the door behind me, and as I saw Grayson, my heart began to slowly crumble.

"Grayson, oh my God, are you alright? Are you sure you want to be here?" I ran towards him.

"I have to be here. I promised my family I would be here. My dad's in meetings with your parents for the rest of the day." He wiped tears from his eyes.

"I can't believe this is where she died. I can't believe this is the last room my baby sister ever saw." His head dropped as he continued to cry in my arms.

"She's in a better place, Grayson. We are going to find Ethan and Violet. They're going to pay for what they did to her. I promise you."

"I want to rip your cousin's throat out with my bare hands." He looked up at me with burning purple eyes.

"I want to torture him for hours on end. I want everyone to see what happens when you mess with my family," he continued.

"Grayson, I know you're in a tremendous amount of pain, but we will think of the proper punishment for the pair of them together," Camila added.

"You don't get to tell me what we will or can do about this. She was a Dark Fae. She was my sister!" he shouted back.

He fell back down into my arms and began sobbing uncontrollably.

"Alexia, you should probably go with Camila. I'm gonna be here for a while," I whispered to my sister. She nodded.

"Very well then, Aria, we will be with your parents if you need us. We'll leave you two alone," Camila's soft voice calmed me.

I stayed there still, holding onto Grayson. The guy who had been strong, who had been my rock since the day I met him, had been turned to mush. I could see the pain he felt with every tear drop that ran down his cheek.

"Ar-Aria. I don't know what I'm going to do. I need my sister. She was my world. She's why I wanted to be the next Dark Fae leader. She's the reason I am the way I am," he cried out.

"I'm so sorry, Grayson."

"She was just a kid! She was a freaking kid in school. How could this happen?"

"Camila's right, Grayson. We will find Ethan and Violet, together. You know they're hiding with Sebastian. There's no way you can take them on by yourself. Let us help you."

"I hate them! Why would they kill her? What did she do to them? She hadn't even gone through her Reckoning."

Before I could answer him, my cell phone started to ring. I pulled the phone out of my pocket and saw that it was a private caller.

"He-hello?" I answered the call and heard someone breathing heavily into the phone.

CHAPTER EIGHTEEN

We walked out of the morgue and waited in a group while the guards brought our cars to us.

"Grayson, do you think if it's okay that I ride with you? I don't want you to be alone." I reached for his hand and he pulled away.

"No, thanks. I will be with my dad and Camila. I think you should ride with your family and him." He pointed at Hunter.

"Are you seriously throwing a tantrum about Hunter? I just met him today. He's my hired guard, for God's sake!"

"He looks at you like you're a glass of water and he's dying of dehydration."

"Grayson, this is crazy. I'm not going to argue about this with you right now. You're not thinking clearly. I'll see you at the school."

"Nah, I don't think I'm going to go. I'm going to have them drop me off at home on the way." He pulled his cell phone out of his pocket and started to text someone.

"For real? You're going to go home when we were just told that Ethan and Violet killed your sister?"

"Yeah, I'm serious. You should go though. After all, they are your family members."

"Grayson, what the hell is your problem? Why are you taking out your anger on me? I haven't done anything!" I shoved his shoulder and felt my eyes start to radiate with fury.

"I-I don't know, Aria. I was told my sister died and then you showed up here, but when I was going to go up to you, I saw you smiling at him." He nodded his head towards Hunter.

"Grayson, I—"

"You don't have to explain anything to me. I know I'm probably overreacting to nothing, but the way he looks at you. It is something. I'm telling you."

"Grayson, I only want you. If you think he looks at me a certain way, just know that I'm only looking at you." I grabbed his hand and squeezed it tightly. The sparks that used to scare me felt warm and welcoming. He leaned closer to me and then kissed me.

"Alright, I love you, Aria. And I'm sorry."

"I love you too, Grayson."

A couple of seconds later, a guy's deep voice broke up our kiss.

"Um, Aria? Our car is here, we should get going."

Without turning around, I knew that it was Hunter speaking. I slowly opened my eyes and saw that Grayson was staring back at me.

"You all should get going, Aria. I'll see you at the school."

CHAPTER NINETEEN

"Hello? Who is this?"

Ethan's voice broke the silence and my body began to burn with anger.

"Hey cuz, did you all find our little present?"

"What the hell is your problem? Why did you kill her?"

Grayson's eyes lit up as he wiped his tears away. "Aria, give me the phone!"

I handed Grayson the phone and when our hands touched, I felt his anger swarm through my body.

"Where are you, coward? Why did you kill a little girl? Why didn't you pick on someone your own size?"

Grayson put the phone on speaker and set it down on a water heater and then punched the brick wall.

"I'm not a coward, I'm smart. I have crippled you without even touching you, idiot."

"You haven't crippled a damn thing! You just woke a sleeping giant. I'm going to kill you."

Ethan's creepy laugh made my blood boil. I felt my body begin to glow.

I butted in, "Ethan, you have no idea what you have done. You're going to have the Dark Royals and my family after you. Why are you helping them? Why are you helping your mom?"

"Cuz, you can't be that dumb. She's my mom. And it's not about helping her. It's about helping Sebastian. Why can't you see that us hiding from the mundanes does no good?"

"Ethan, you can't be that stupid! Sebastian doesn't want the Fae to just come out from hiding. He is going to want to eliminate the humans and then he'll put the Light and Dark at war with each other. He's a selfish prick!"

Grayson's eyes were flashing a bright violet as he added, "Ethan, I swear to you right now: I will kill you and your mom."

Ethan's laugh was a little more nervous now and then he mumbled, "Aria, don't be dumb. Join us and ditch them, while you can."

Before I could respond, my cousin hung up the phone.

Grayson grabbed the phone from the water heater and threw it across the room.

"I swear to God! I am going to kill him!"

"Let's find him together and then decide what to do. If we can get to him, it'll make it easier for us to get to Violet and Sebastian."

He nodded as he pulled his phone out from his pocket and began to text someone.

"Who are you texting?"

"My brothers. I'm going to meet up with them. Hopefully they've been able to track down your cousin and aunt somehow."

"Want me to come with you?"

"Nah, it's alright. I'll call you later if I find anything else out. You should go see if our parents have been able to get any information."

"Alright, and I'll do the same—I'll call you if there's anything new."

He looked up at me and I could see that there was only pain in his eyes.

"And Grayson, I love you, okay?"

"I know. I love you, too."

CHAPTER TWENTY

I walked Grayson back to his car and then went back into the school's meeting room.

Alexia greeted me as everyone else was arguing about Sebastian Harper.

"Hey, where's Grayson? Is he alright?"

"He went to meet up with Briar and Cayne. I don't think he'll be alright for a long time. What's going on here? Anything new on Sebastian and Violet?"

My sister shook her head.

I leaned closer to her and whispered, "Ethan called me when we were in the basement."

"Are you kidding me? What did he want?" Her eyes widened and began to glow blue.

"He said that he's helping Sebastian cripple the Dark Royals and a bunch of other crap. Do you think that I should tell them?" I pointed at my family and Grayson's parents.

"Yeah, you probably should. Maybe it'll get them to shut up about who's doing their job and who isn't."

My sister and I walked towards the group of people and not one of them paid us any attention.

I cleared my throat, "Um, Ethan just called me."

Everyone immediately quit talking and then looked at me.

Camila spoke first. "What did he say? Why didn't you call one of us?"

Cherise added, "Where's Grayson? Was he with you when Ethan called?"

"The call was quick, I didn't really think about running up here to get you guys. I just wanted to know why Ethan did it. And Grayson went to meet with Briar and Cayne."

Cherise began to cry as Mr. Treble consoled her. I continued, "Ethan said that he's helping Sebastian take control over the Fae. He wants the Fae to be out and walking in the public among mundanes."

Camila sighed. "My ex-husband has always wanted the Fae to be equals among the mundanes. He continues to forget that the last time we tried that, we lost hundreds of our kind. Mundanes are not good with feeling inferior to anyone. They're not okay with change."

My dad added, "The Fae people are not in hiding because we're scared. We hide from the humans to protect ourselves. We cannot allow them to try and capture us and use us as their pets. Can you imagine going to a Fae-filled circus?"

Everyone was silent as my dad continued, "Can you imagine how this world would go up in flames if Fae and mundanes worked together? They have their wars and if we walked among them, they'd force us to choose a side. We do not want another Fae war."

Braden, Grayson's dad, spoke now, "I agree with you, Liam. A Fae war would be a disaster for all of us."

Camila took a long sip of her drink and then said, "The Fae war was promoted as positive propaganda from my delusional ex-husband. Believe it or not, some of the Light Fae began to believe some of his lies. We cannot allow him to divide us all. I know that emotions are high today, but what happened here is no one's fault except Violet, Ethan, and Sebastian."

Everyone stayed quiet for a second and Camila continued, "Aria, from what I gather, you have heard of the Destructive Fire, is that correct?"

My parents held their breath as I slowly responded to her, "Ye-yes. Grayson and I feel it when we touch each other."

"Well, just so we are all clear, the rumors are true. The Light Fae were cursed and any time the Destructive Fire is felt, those two are doomed to fail."

"I'm not a Light Fae though!" I protested.

"I know, and that's what makes your situation so unique. You are the first of your kind, as I was the first Light Fae. You felt the fire before your reckoning, so your heart knew you wanted to be Light. But you fought against your heart and quite frankly, against the universe. Sebastian doesn't know how to react to you. You're somewhat of an anomaly."

"Did your cousin tell you why he did it? Why did he choose our baby girl?" Braden asked, fighting back his tears.

"Um, not exactly. He just bragged about hurting you all," I hesitantly responded.

Camila's aura was radiating with anger and could be felt throughout the room. "Ethan would not have done this on his own. He was following orders from Sebastian and Violet. Sebastian doesn't do a lot of his dirty work; he has others do it for him."

My dad stood up and signaled for my mom to join him. "Mr. and Mrs. Treble, you have our family's support. I can't imagine the pain you all are feeling. I guarantee you, the Light Fae guards will be on the hunt for Ethan."

My mom added, "I agree with my husband. I want you all to know that just because I was related to Violet once, it will not stop us from hunting her and my disgusting nephew down. They will pay for this."

Cherise nodded and walked over to hug my mom. I heard her whisper, "Thank you, Adalyn."

Mr. Treble cleared his throat. "Cherise, let's head home. You need to get some rest, and I've got a meeting with some of our guards."

My dad agreed with him, "Yes, we should be going, too. I will let you know if we hear anything, Braden."

CHAPTER TWENTY-ONE

I rode back to our house with my sister and my guard, Hunter. Alexia whispered, "Aria, I seriously can't get over how hot he is. Like, why couldn't he be my guard?"

I felt my face blush and as I looked up, I saw that Hunter was grinning from ear to ear. I decided to tease him, since he was obviously listening to our conversation. "Yeah, he's alright. But have you noticed how strange he smells?"

Alexia hit me and I laughed when Hunter turned around to snap at us. "Can you two be normal for two minutes?"

I mumbled, "Someone didn't like my comment, huh?"

My sister was blushing now. "I guess not. I mean, he doesn't smell though, does he?"

Instead of going on about Hunter, I pulled my cell

phone out of my bag and texted Grayson:

Hey. I'm on my way home. You alright?

Alexia's phone buzzed. I looked at her, "Who's texting you?"

She glanced at her phone and then stared back at me. "Um, it's Briar. He says that Grayson hasn't made it home. He thinks he's out looking for Ethan on his own."

"Are you kidding? Have they tried calling him?" I immediately picked my phone back up and began to call him.

Dammit, Grayson. Pick up the phone.

Alexia put her arm on me. I immediately pulled my arm away as I felt her cold touch.

"Aria, calm down. I'm sure he's alright. You have to keep your cool. You're freaking out."

I looked down at my skin and saw that I was glowing bright with different shades of purple and blue.

I put my phone down, took a deep breath, and closed my eyes.

"Alexia, give me your phone. I need to call Briar."

She hesitantly handed me her phone and I before I

dialed his number, I saw that he had heart emojis by his name. I raised my eyebrow at her and then hit dial.

He picked up in less than three rings, "Hey, what's up?"

"Um, Briar, it's Aria. Have you had any luck getting ahold of Grayson?"

"Oh, uh, hey, Aria. No, we haven't been able to track him either. My parents just got home and the guards are getting them updated. We think he's out looking for Ethan."

I squeezed the phone tightly with frustration. "Briar, we're on our way to your house. We've got to find Grayson. I don't want him to go after Ethan or Violet alone."

I hung up before he could respond and told Hunter to drive us to the Dark Royals.

CHAPTER TWENTY-TWO

Hunter stopped the car and turned around to look at Alexia and me. "I don't think we should be going to the Dark Royals without your parents, Aria."

"Hunter, I'm sorry, but I think you work for me. Take me there, now."

Alexia hit my arm. "Aria, don't be so rude."

Hunter's jawline tightened as his eyes began to glow a light blue. "Aria, I don't work for you. I work for your parents. If you want to go to the Dark Royals' home, you'll have to get there on your own."

"Alright, get me home. I'll get a car on my own."

Hunter grabbed his phone and dialed my dad's phone. "Sir, I just wanted to inform you that Aria is requesting that I drive them to the Dark Royals."

My dad was on speaker phone and sounded furious. "Aria, you need to get home. The Trebles have enough on their hands. They don't need you meddling around in their business."

"Dad, I am going to go. I can either go with Alexia and Hunter, or I can go by myself. I have to go. Grayson didn't ever make it home and they can't track him."

My dad let out a long, exhausted sigh. "Hunter, take care of my girls. If there's any sort of danger, get them out of there immediately. You'll know what you'll have to do."

Hunter turned back around and started the car again.

I looked at my sister. "What do you think dad meant, he knows what he'll have to do?"

She shrugged her shoulders and continued to text someone on her phone.

"Alexia, why do you have heart emojis by Briar's name?"

"No reason. Quit being nosey, Aria."

I smiled at her and then nervously called Grayson again.

"Dammit, why aren't you answering the phone? Where are you? Call me back as soon as you get this!"

I dialed over and over again but had no luck. Hunter broke the awkward silence that had built up in the car. "We're here. Before you all get off, promise me that neither of you will run off without me. It is my job to keep you both protected. Specifically you, Aria."

I nodded and pushed open my door.

CHAPTER TWENTY-THREE

Briar and his twin, Cayne, met Alexia and me at the door. Briar hugged Alexia a second longer than normal and Cayne and I just smiled at them until they separated.

Briar stuttered, "Uh, um, yeah, so my parents gave us the okay to go look for Grayson—as long as we stay together. They have trackers out trying to find him, but they've been pretty unlucky."

I asked, "Does anyone even know where to start looking? I mean, it's not like we know where Violet and Ethan are staying. I don't know how Grayson would be able to find them before all of the other trackers."

"Why don't we go look at your spot? You know, where you had your reckoning," Cayne mumbled.

We all looked at each other and I hugged Cayne a little too tightly. "Perfect! He's not out looking for them. He's there. He has to be. He wants to be away from the world. We've got to get there, quick."

I turned around and saw Hunter standing a few feet behind us. He did not look pleased with my plan.

"Aria, do you think it's smart that we go into the middle of nowhere, especially now that it's getting dark out?"

"Are you afraid of the dark, Hunter?" I teased him.

"Not at all. But I don't think it's smart for us to go running through the dark with Violet, Ethan, and Sebastian out there."

"If we run into them, we won't be the ones that are scared. We will be fine. Do you want to drive us, or do you want to follow us?"

"I'll drive you. I don't need you trying to shake me off."

Briar, Cayne, Alexia, and I loaded into the car and headed towards the forest where my reckoning had been held.

–

The closer we got to Grayson's and my special place, the more nervous I got.

"Aria, I'm sure he's alright. I don't know why we didn't think to come look here in the first place.

He probably just wanted to escape from the world, ya 'know?" my sister tried to comfort me with her words.

"I hope he's here. And I hope we get to him before Ethan or Violet figure out where he might be."

"Uh, should we all get out and see if he's here, or do you want to get out alone, Aria?" Hunter put the car in park as he turned around and looked at me.

Alexia answered before I could. "Why don't we all get out but Aria goes in alone?"

I nodded in agreement with her plan and the five of us got out of the car. I had just started to walk closer to our hidden nook when rain started pouring down from the sky. I turned back around and looked at Hunter, Cayne, Briar, and Alexia.

Hunter put his finger over his mouth, signaling for me to be quiet when Alexia whispered, "Do you think it's an Elemental doing this?"

CHAPTER TWENTY-FOUR

Cayne put his hands out, and his eyes lit up a bright violet. As his hand ran through the rain, the water steamed off his now glowing hand.

Cayne took a fighting stance, which automatically caused the rest of us to join him. He mumbled, "It's an Elemental, alright. This is not rain from our dear friend, Mother Nature."

Hunter's eyes were glowing violently as he was now standing by my side. "Aria, we should get out of here. We don't know how many of them there are."

I felt my eyes burning with an intense glow when I heard Grayson's voice from inside of the nook, "Aria, get out of here!"

I started to run towards the nook yelling, "Grayson! Grayson! Are you okay?"

Hunter wrapped his arms around me, stopping me

just a few feet away from Grayson. "Aria, you heard him, we need to get out of here!"

Cayne and Briar were at our side now. "Hunter, get the girls out of here. We'll go in."

"Let go of me, dammit!" I struggled to get out of Hunter's arms.

I felt my body begin to burn and as I looked down at my hand and saw that it was lit up in the now familiar shades of blue, purple, and green.

"Dammit, Aria!" Hunter let me go and started to rub his hands.

Alexia walked over to Hunter and me. "Her touch get a little too warm for you, huh?"

I smiled and continued to the nook with Cayne and Briar.

I could hear Grayson's strained voice from the other side of the door. "Aria, don't come in here. Violet just left. Go find her!"

The hairs on my body stood up as he said Violet's name. I turned to look at Hunter and Alexia. "You two call Mom and Dad. Tell them where we are. Start looking around for Violet."

Hunter looked at me hesitantly. "Aria, we shouldn't split up."

"Do it, now!"

He nodded and ran back towards the car with Alexia.

I looked at Cayne and Briar and then opened the door to the nook.

My heart sunk into my stomach as I saw blood dripping down Grayson's face.

CHAPTER TWENTY-FIVE

"Grayson, Grayson, are you alright? What happened?" I rushed past Briar and Cayne, who were pale-faced.

Grayson was holding onto an open gash on his forehead with one hand and a cut on his arm with the other. "I came here to get away—to think about everything and what it all means. I was sitting out on the hilltop when rain started pouring down. I came inside and when I closed the door, Violet and Ethan were here, waiting for me. Ethan held me down as Violet tied me up."

I looked to the left of him and saw that there was a broken chair with worn rope lying next to it.

Cayne walked towards the back room and then was quickly at our sides again with a first aid kit. "Briar, call dad. He needs to get some of our guards here, now."

Briar nodded and stepped outside.

"What did they want? Why did they do this to you?" I asked.

"They wanted me to join them. They wanted me to help them kill Camila."

"What do you mean they want to kill Camila? Why?"

He shrugged. "Ouch."

"Don't move, you idiot. You've lost a lot of blood already. Give me a couple of minutes and I'll have you patched up," Cayne said.

I walked around the broken chair and asked, "How did they ask you to join them? They didn't tell you anything? I mean, why do they all of a sudden want to kill Camila?"

"Aria, chill out with the twenty questions. I don't know. I don't know why they want to kill Camila. Maybe because she's the Original Light Fae and is one of three people who can stop them," Grayson said, irritated.

"What do you mean one of three people?"

He looked at me and let out a long sigh. "I mean, Sebastian is the Original Dark Fae, Camila is the Original Light Fae, and you're the Original, well, you."

Before I could respond, Briar walked back inside. "Cayne, the guards are on their way."

"Did you see Alexia and Hunter out there?" I asked.

Briar nodded. "Yeah, um, about that. They just drove back up."

"Okay?"

"They were going to check out the area like you asked, and they said that we're barricaded here."

Grayson growled, "Briar, what the hell do you mean we're barricaded here?"

Alexia walked in. "Holy shit, you guys. There are uprooted trees all the way around us. There's no way we can get past them without a little help."

CHAPTER TWENTY-SIX

Briar, Cayne, and I ran outside to see what Alexia was talking about, while she stayed behind to watch over Grayson.

I saw Hunter was on his phone and hanging out a couple hundred feet ahead of us. I started to jog towards him. "Hey, Hunter! What's going on?"

Hunter turned around as I approached him, and he hung up the phone. "Your dad is on the way with some of our guards. I know that Briar called the Dark guards, but it's going to take a lot more power than what they've got to get these trees up."

I looked around and saw hundreds of large Angel Oak trees lying flat on the ground. The large branches that were usually sturdy and erect, were now down, damaged. "There's no way Violet and Ethan could have done this alone. I mean, they're strong but this would've taken them far too long."

Hunter went on, "Yeah that's what I was thinking. The trees are like this all the way around us. Alexia and I looked for an opening so we could try and track them, but we're stuck. We managed to move one tree, but that nearly wiped us out."

Briar and Cayne finally walked up to us, a little out of breath. Cayne looked sad. "All of these trees, probably hundreds of years old, now lying here, dead."

"Do you think that Sebastian did this?" I asked.

Briar touched the ground and then looked up at the damp sky. I don't think Sebastian was here. I'm getting quite a few different Fae imprints here."

"Are you saying Fae, other than Violet and Ethan, did this?" Hunter asked.

Briar nodded, "Yeah, I'd say there was about ten to fifteen different Fae."

"How's that possible?" Cayne asked.

I looked around us and saw Grayson was limping towards us with Alexia's help. "They're building an army."

Cayne's face turned pale. "Who would join those lunatics? What type of Fae would do this? A natural Fae knows that disrespecting Mother Nature like this is just asking for trouble."

"I think that the Fae who helped kidnap your sister have gotten some of their friends to help out," Hunter added.

Grayson was suddenly at his brothers' sides and leaned on Briar. "Holy shit."

Briar let out a small laugh, "Yeah, I know. This isn't even the half of it."

Grayson looked at Briar, Cayne, and then at me. "What do you mean?"

"Uh, we think Violet and Ethan are growing an army of rogue Fae."

CHAPTER TWENTY-SEVEN

Alexia laughed, "You've got to be kidding me. Like, you're seriously joking, right? I mean, a rogue army of Fae?"

No one returned the laughter and then the smile from her face disappeared. "You all really believe that's what this is?" She pointed at the large trees that were lying lifeless on the ground.

"I mean, it makes sense. And Briar said that there were at least ten to fifteen Fae here," Cayne said.

"Do you think that it's all Dark Fae?" Alexia asked.

Briar shook his head, "That's the scary part. I wouldn't be surprised if it were disgruntled Dark Fae, but I can sense some Light Fae affinities as well."

Grayson looked at me and then asked, "Can you sense the Light Fae imprints?"

I shook my head, "I don't know how to do that."

Cayne circled around me. "You've never tried, but I bet you can definitely see imprints."

Hunter butted in, "How are you so sure?"

"Probably because she's Aria," Alexia added.

I looked at the group and saw that all of their eyes were lit up in their respective colors, curiously staring back at me.

"What should I do? I mean, if I knew how to read imprints, what would I see?" I asked.

Briar took my hand and walked me over to a fallen tree. "Well, first off, you've got to close your eyes and clear your mind. You basically have to tell your mind that you're looking for imprints."

I closed my eyes and put my hand on the ground in front of the tree.

After a few seconds, I stood back up. "I got nothing. I told myself, look for imprints. I saw nothing."

Briar pulled me back towards the ground by my arm.

"Uh, that was my arm, not a twig, Briar," I said, aggravated.

"Shut up, Aria. Close your eyes and try. Actually try to look for an imprint."

"What does an imprint even look like?"

He sighed, "You know how when you close your eyes really tight, you start to see little white specks that begin to look like stars?"

I nodded, "Yeah, I guess."

He ignored my pessimism. "Alright, well it is sort of similar. Only with imprints, even though every Fae has a unique imprint, you can tell if they're Light or Dark by seeing smudges of blue or purple."

"You mean smudges like smeared paint?" I asked.

"Exactly like that. The more vibrant the color shows, the stronger the Fae."

I closed my eyes.

Almost instantly, bright shades of blue and purple were surrounding me. I opened my eyes, and I could see the blue smudges all over the fallen trees.

CHAPTER TWENTY-EIGHT

Just moments after I noticed the bright blue imprints on the trees, warm tears started falling down my cheek.

I looked at everyone who was staring at me and Alexia asked, "Aria, what is it? What did you see?"

"Light Fae were here. The Light Fae were responsible for the Fallen Angel Oak trees. They're helping the rogue Dark Fae."

Briar nodded in agreement, "Yeah, I saw the same. Although the Light Fae imprints are not as bright as the purple imprints."

Hunter looked at his cell phone and then mumbled, "Uh, so, what should I tell your dad? Because he's calling."

I took the phone from Hunter. "Give me the phone."

I answered the phone and before I could tell my dad that I had Hunter's phone, he was talking, "Hunter, we are on the other side of the Oak Trees. This is crazy, are you all okay?"

"Uh, dad. It's me."

"Is Hunter there? Is he alright? Why do you have his phone?"

"Everything is fine. I took the phone from him. Dad, do you have guards with you?"

"Of course I do, why would you ask that, Aria? What's going on?"

"The trees were taken down by Light Fae. Is Camila at the house?"

My dad stayed quiet for a second. "Yeah, she's home with guards outside of her door. How do you know Light Fae did this? Why would they do this?"

"I saw their imprints here."

A low growl came from the other side of the phone, "What do you mean, you saw their imprints?"

"I mean, I can see imprints and Light Fae were involved. Don't trust anyone. We think Violet and

Sebastian are building an army of rogue Fae."

"Aria, don't say a word of this to anyone. We'll get through the trees soon. Love you."

"Love you, too."

I hung up the phone and saw that everyone was staring at me.

Alexia asked, "Is dad alright?"

I nodded, "Yeah, he's alright. Camila is too. They're breaking through the trees now."

Grayson held up his phone. "Our guards are here too. Let's see who breaks through first, huh?"

Briar was by Grayson's side and started looking up at the sky.

Cayne looked at his twin, at me, and then at the sky.

I looked up and saw that there was lightning in the clouds and I closed my eyes to focus on the bright bolts as they went off.

There were long streaks of purple and blue that looked like smeared paint across the sky.

I opened my eyes. "How is that possible?"

Briar met my stare and then looked at Cayne. "The

weather is being affected by a Fae, not Mother Nature."

Hunter stepped closer to me. "Do you think it's the same Fae that were here?"

Briar and I nodded.

"Yeah, but this time there are a lot more of them," I said.

CHAPTER TWENTY-NINE

Hunter grabbed his phone from me and then started calling someone.

"Who are you calling?" I asked.

"I'm calling your dad. He should not be here. We don't know who we can trust and I don't want him to be harmed."

"He has guards with him," Alexia added.

"Yeah, but can we really risk it? We don't know who the good and bad guys are anymore, Alexia," Hunter grunted.

I whispered to Cayne as Hunter kept trying to get ahold of my dad, "Are your parents here?"

He shook his head, "Nah. They're basically on lockdown at the house. No one in or out unless they're vetted by my dad's main guard."

Grayson spoke now, "Aria, your dad's the new

Light Fae leader. There really isn't anyone he can really trust, is there?"

I looked over at Hunter and then back at Grayson. "I think the only person he can trust besides my mom and Camila, is him."

Hunter finally got my dad on the phone. "Dammit, sir. I've been trying to get ahold of you. You need to get back to the house immediately."

Hunter's face turned red and then his eyes lit up with a blue fury.

"What's going on?" Alexia asked.

He put his finger over his lips, signaling for her to shut up.

A couple of seconds later, he hung up the phone and shoved it back in his jeans.

"I swear to God, Aria. Now I know where you get your stubbornness from. It's so damn annoying."

I let out a quiet giggle. "Um, is everything alright?"

"Your dad was refusing to leave. They're about to clear a path right over there."

He pointed about one hundred feet away from where we were standing and as if on cue, some of the fallen trees began to move around. We looked at each other and then ran towards the new opening.

I was the first one there and immediately ran into my dad's arms.

"Oh baby, I was so worried. I'm glad you all alright. Where's your sister?"

Alexia quickly joined us and then pointed at Grayson and Briar, who were still a few feet behind her. "Dad, we've got to get Grayson some help. He was injured pretty badly."

My dad's eyes lit up blue. He looked at Grayson and then at me. "Was this Violet's doing?"

I nodded as Grayson limped up to us. "Hey, Mr. Whitelace. Nice of you to join us."

CHAPTER THIRTY

"Hey Grayson, nice to see you. How are you holding up?" my dad asked.

"Eh, under the circumstances I guess I'd say that I'm alright," Grayson teased.

Hunter greeted my dad with annoyance still in his voice, "Mr. Whitelace, I really wish you wouldn't have come today. You're the leader of the Light Fae; you need to be at the house, safe. Not here, on the front lines of an attack."

My dad patted Hunter on the shoulder. "Hunter, you forget that I was once a –guard. I know I look like an old man, but hey, I've still got my hair—and it's not gray."

The guards around my dad started laughing as we heard a rumble come from the trees behind us, behind Grayson's and my hidden nook. All of the guards' eyes immediately turned to a bright, glowing blue, and they were on the defensive, surrounding us.

Hunter took the lead and signaled for the rest of the guards to escort us away.

Cayne's phone started ringing and he stepped out of the protective circle to answer it.

A few moments later, Cayne shouted out, "It's alright Hunter, stand down. It's just the Dark guards. I just got a call. They're breaking through the trees now."

The guards around us stayed in their defensive positions as a bright purple light blinded us. As I refocused my eyes, I saw a swarm of black SUVs coming through.

Briar shouted, "It's the guards, everyone can calm down."

Briar and Cayne pushed Hunter out of the way and started waving their hands to signal the guards.

The fleet of SUVs parked just feet away from us and a tall, dark-skinned man walked out. "Briar, Cayne, Grayson, your father asks that you come with us immediately."

I looked at Cayne, curious. "Who's that?"

"My dad's lead guard," Cayne mumbled.

Hunter walked closer to the tall man and reached

to shake his hand. "I'm Hunter Spark, guard for the Light Family."

The man looked surprised at Hunter's warm greeting and showed a small smile. "I'm Andre Legion, head guard for the Dark Royals. Thank you for keeping the boys safe until we were able to get here. The Angel Oaks gave my guys some serious problems."

"Yeah, I think it gave ours some trouble, too. These are some strong trees, but the guys should not have had that much of a problem getting through."

Andre looked around and then stared up at the sky. "This was a combination attack? Light and Dark Fae working together?"

Briar cut into the conversation, "Yes, that's right. Violet and Ethan are the two who hurt Grayson, but they had the help of Light and Dark Fae to pull the Angel Oaks out of the ground.

Andre's eyes lit up violet. "We need to get you boys home. Your dad's worried sick."

Grayson walked closer to me. "I'll call you later? I probably should go get some rest, huh?"

I leaned in and kissed him on the cheek. "Yeah, go get some rest. Just call me tomorrow. I'm a little tired myself."

Andre reached out to shake Hunter's hand again. "Thank you, Hunter. I'm sure we will see each other again."

Cayne, Briar, and Grayson followed Andre back to the SUV he had previously stepped out of. Before Grayson got into the vehicle, he waved at me with a small grin, and his beautiful eyes lit up a bright violet.

CHAPTER THIRTY-ONE

When we got back to the house, my mom and Camila were sitting in the dining room. As soon as they saw Alexia and me, they immediately got up and walked towards us.

"My babies, I've been so sick and worried about you two. Thank God you're okay." My mom hugged us so tight that I had to tap her arm to remind her I wasn't a stuffed animal.

"Mom, we're okay. We're here. Grayson's the one who was hurt," I said.

"What do you mean, Grayson was hurt? How?" Camila asked.

I walked back towards the table where my mom and Camila had just been sitting. "Can we get some tea?" I asked.

"Yes, of course." My mom began to pour Alexia and me each a drink as I continued to tell them what happened with Grayson.

"Violet and Ethan somehow got into the nook and tied Grayson down. They hurt him pretty badly and were asking him to join them." I looked around nervously.

"Join them for what?" my mom asked.

"Well, uh, they wanted Grayson to help them kill you." I pointed at Camila.

She let out a laugh, "My goodness, those two are clueless. How do they think that either of them is strong enough to kill me?"

I shrugged my shoulders.

Alexia added, "Tell them the rest…"

I glared at her.

My mom asked, "What else happened, Aria?"

"Uh, so I can see Fae imprints now."

Mom nearly choked on her tea as Camila's eyes began to show a light golden glow.

"Is that right? How did you find out that you had that capability?" Camila asked.

"After we got Grayson a little help, his brother Briar kind of showed me how. We were surrounded by Angel Oak trees that had been up-rooted. He was showing me how to tell who was responsible for it."

"Were you able to identify the Fae?" Camila questioned.

"No. There were too many different imprints."

Alexia huffed, "Aria, why are you beating around the bush? Tell them everything."

I threw a napkin at her. "I'm getting there, give me a second. I'm a little tired."

"Like I was saying," I glared at my sister, "there were a lot of different imprints. They weren't just Dark imprints either—"

Camila cut me off, "Are you suggesting that Light Fae were involved with Violet's plan?"

I nodded.

My mom's face was red with anger and confusion when my dad walked into the room. "I'm sorry I didn't come right in, Adalyn. I needed to make sure that Declan had plenty of security."

My dad hugged my mom and then smiled at Camila. "By the look on your faces, I take it that Aria filled you in on the latest and greatest, huh?"

"Liam, you knew about all of this and you didn't think for a second to call me on your way home?" my mom scolded my dad.

"Ah, Adalyn. I didn't want you freaking out while I wasn't here to explain what our plan of action is. I was talking to Hunter and—"

My mom stood up, put her hand up, and stopped my dad mid-sentence. "Liam Whitelace, do not forget that we are the Light Fae family. We are the leaders. You are not alone in the decision making. How dare you come up with some sort of plan of action without me!"

My dad's face turned red from either embarrassment or anger; it was kind of hard to tell. "You're right. I'm sorry. I just thought it'd be better for you to hear it from us in person and not over the phone."

Camila butted into the conversation, "I'm sorry, Liam, but I agree with Adalyn on this one. Whatever plan of action you have decided to take should have been run by her. She is just as much the leader of the Light as you are. And I'm sorry, but creating some sort of knee-jerk reaction to what happened is just what my ex-husband would want from you all."

Alexia mumbled, "So what are we going to do?

We have to figure out who we can and can't trust. If some of the Light Fae were involved, don't you think it'd be smart of us to make sure it's no one from inside this house?"

Camila nodded in agreement, "Alexia, I agree with you. I say we begin questioning everyone immediately. What do you think, Adalyn?"

My mom looked at Alexia and me, then at my dad. "Let's begin with all of our personal guards. The questioning must take place in the sacred room. They will not be able to get away with lying there."

We all looked at my dad, who cleared his throat after a couple of seconds. "Very well, then. It looks like I've been outnumbered. I'll get Hunter to gather our guards. Interrogations will begin first thing tomorrow."

CHAPTER
THIRTY-TWO

I called Grayson when I woke up the next day. "Hey, how are you feeling?"

"I'm alright, I'm a little sore but that's not a big deal."

I began combing my hair and holding up different tops in front of my large mirror. "I know I sound like a total girl right now, but what does one wear to an interrogation?"

He laughed, "I don't think that this is a conversation mundanes go through."

I giggled, "Yeah, I guess you're right. I guess I should be asking what I should wear to school, but we all know me going to a mundane school is over with."

"You're not going back?"

"Nah, after everything that's happened, my parents think I should just do the whole home school thing. And I don't think it's a bad idea."

"Whoa. A few months ago you were so gung-ho on going to a mundane school and being normal. Now you're this homegirl Fae who makes her own rules."

"Yeah, I guess when your aunt and cousin want to kill you that kind of changes things."

He laughed, "My parents are going to do their own kind of interrogations today as well. I think our parents are meeting tonight for dinner. Are you coming with them?"

I blushed and sat down on my vanity chair. "Um, I don't know. Maybe."

"Maybe? Really? Come on, I want to see you."

I felt my eyes glow with excitement as the butterflies in my stomach began to flutter. "Really? You just saw me yesterday."

"Aria…" Grayson said with a little irritation.

"I've got to go. I'll see if I can fit this dinner into my schedule," I teased.

"Alright. Talk to you later."

"Bye, Grayson."

He hung up and I stared at my phone. Alexia walked into my room wearing a long black sundress with a large black hat.

"Aria, are you ready for the interrogations?"

"Grayson hung up on me without saying bye." I stayed staring at my phone's blank screen.

"Oh god, get over it. Get dressed. Let's find out who these traitors are."

I stared at my phone and then at my sister again. "I'm almost done. I just have to get a shirt on. Are you dressed?"

She looked at herself in the mirror, adjusting her hat. "Yup, do you love it?"

"Uh, not really. You're dressed for a funeral. We're doing an interrogation."

"Whatever. Get dressed. I'll meet you in the kitchen. Mom's cooking breakfast."

My sister walked out of my room and I texted Grayson:

I'm going tonight. Don't ever hang up on me again. See you later.

CHAPTER THIRTY-THREE

I walked into the kitchen and saw that I was the last person to get there. My dad smiled at me and then pointed at the empty chair between him and Camila.

"Sit, Aria. As soon as we're done eating, we're going to meet Hunter in the interrogation rooms." My dad began to pour coffee into his usual mug.

"You sleep well, Aria?" Camila asked.

"Yeah, I didn't realize how sleepy I was. I was pretty much knocked out."

Alexia was sitting across from me. She reached over for the biscuits. "How's Grayson doing? Why did he hang up on you?"

I felt my eyes widen. "He's alright. I was teasing him about not going over with you all tonight and I don't think he was in the joking mood."

Camila smiled at me, "Ah, to be young again."

My mom laughed. "Liam, who will be conducting the interrogations this morning?"

"Hunter will be leading the interrogations on our main guards, and then we will join them to interview the others."

My dad looked at me and then asked, "Speaking of the Trebles, do you know if they're holding their interrogations this morning?"

I nodded and continued to eat.

"Well, that's good. I hope by the time we meet this evening, we all know who's betraying us."

Camila agreed, "Well, I hope that by this evening, we'll have an idea where Violet and my ex-husband are hiding."

Hunter walked into the room. "Mr. Whitelace, we're all ready for the interrogations upstairs."

My dad stood up. "Very well then, did everyone show up?"

Hunter nodded, "The immediate guards did. The secondaries are not set to report here until noon."

I asked, "Hunter, do you think that any of our immediate guards are involved?"

Hunter looked at my dad and Camila before answering me.

I pushed on, annoyed. "Hunter, I asked you a question. Do you think it's our immediate guards involved?"

My dad answered for him, "Aria, we're not sure who's involved. That's why we're interrogating everyone."

"How are we going to know if someone is lying?" Alexia asked.

"Why don't we all go upstairs so Hunter can explain the process to all of us?" My dad started to walk towards Hunter.

I took my phone out of my pocket and saw a text from Grayson:

I'll hang up on you whenever I feel like it...jk, don't kill me. See you
  tonight.

I smiled and walked with my family up to the interrogation rooms.

CHAPTER THIRTY-FOUR

The interrogation rooms were all on the same floor and strangely resembled a police station. There were a bunch of desks as you walked in and then private rooms towards the back.

"I feel like I'm in a weird episode of Law and Order," Alexia joked.

"We're going to be in Room One for the first part of the day," Hunter began to explain.

"As we go through the main list of guards, we will ask for them to place their hands on this." He held up a large black box with silver edges.

"What is that?" I asked.

Camila answered for him, "It's the Candor Box."

"The Candor Box?" Alexia asked.

"Yes. When a Fae places their hands on this box, they're unable to lie. They will be forced to tell the truth," Hunter replied.

"The Candor Box is a old Fae artifact. I thought it was destroyed years ago," Camila said in admiration.

"If we have the Candor Box, how are the Dark Fae doing their interrogations?" I asked.

"The Dark Fae have their own interrogation ways. Some would say they're not very … humane," Hunter said.

"Ah, my ex-husband's old tricks seem to have trickled down through the generations, I see," Camila added.

Hunter nodded as he signaled for us to follow him.

"While I do the main interrogations, you all will be behind the two-way glass in that room." He pointed at the door next to Interrogation Room One.

"As the day goes on, I'll be rotating interrogations with some of the other main guards. Hopefully, we will be able to find the traitors sooner rather than later."

I followed my parents into the observation room and before Hunter closed the door, he asked me to join him outside. I looked at my parents and my mom signaled for me to go with him.

I walked back outside into the lobby area with Hunter.

"What's up?" I asked.

"I just want to make sure you know that this could get intense. I just need you to make sure that you'll be able to keep your composure. I can't have you going crazy and blowing things up with your powers," he said.

I laughed.

"I'm being serious, Aria. You've got to promise to keep your cool. No matter what sort of information we find out."

I let out a long sigh and held my pinky out, "I pinky promise."

He smiled at me. "Your dad did my interrogation this morning. The box is the real deal. There's no way anyone will be able to lie while holding it."

He opened the door to the observation room and then closed it behind me.

CHAPTER THIRTY-FIVE

All of the main guards easily passed their interrogations. Hunter joined us in the observation room as we moved on to the secondary interrogations.

Hunter took a seat between me and my mom.

I whispered, "Good job today. Were you nervous?"

He shook his head, "Nah, I felt pretty confident that the main guards were good."

"I'm a bit surprised that there wasn't even one bad apple," Alexia said, joining the conversation.

"This is where things are going to get a little intense," Hunter said, ignoring my sister.

On the other side of the glass window, Jeffrey, another main guard, began his interrogation with the first guard.

"Please place your hands on the Candor Box and state your name for the record," Jeffrey said.

The dark-haired man's eyes lit up blue as his hands touched the box.

"Alexander Bitton," he answered shortly.

"Alexander, do you know why you're here today?" Jeffrey asked.

"N-n-yes," Alexander stuttered and began sweating as his eyes glowed brighter.

"What's happening?" I asked Hunter.

"He tried lying. He knows why he's here."

Jeffrey continued his interrogation, "Very well, then. I guess you've figured out that as long as your hands are on the box, you'll be unable to lie."

The guard nodded.

"And are you aware that there are Light Fae guards helping Violet Whitelace and Sebastian Harper?"

The guard's eyes continued to glow as he stared directly at us.

"Y-yes," he stuttered again and tried to remove his hands from the box.

Jeffrey made a clicking sound with his mouth. "I wouldn't do that if I were you. You may only remove your hands from the box with my permission."

Alexander's face began to turn red.

"Alexander, have you ever come into contact with Violet or Sebastian?" Jeffrey asked.

I didn't realize I was holding my breath until Hunter put his hand on my leg.

"I have not," Alexander responded.

"Do you know if any of your peers have come into contact with Violet or Sebastian?"

We all looked at each other anxiously.

"Ye-yes!" he shouted out. Jeffrey instantly turned back to look at us.

Hunter stood up. "I've got to get in there."

Hunter walked out of the observation room, and a second later he was on the other side of the double-sided glass.

He stood next to Alexander now. "Just so you're aware, I've been watching your interrogation from right there."

Hunter pointed at the glass and the continued, "How many guards are involved with Sebastian and Violet?"

"I only know of two." Alexander's eyes were glowing, and his face continued to turn a bright red.

"Who are they?" Jeffrey demanded.

Alexander's eyes began to water and tears were falling down his cheek. "I cannot say!"

Hunter's eyes lit up and he slammed his hand on the table. "Tell us who the traitors are!"

"I cannot say!" the guard shouted out, in pain now.

Blood began to drip down his cheeks. "Please, make it stop!"

"What's happening?" I asked.

Camila stood up. "Someone's put a bind on him."

"What's a bind?" Alexia asked.

My mom answered as Camila walked out of the observation room. "It's sort of like an invisible muzzle. If he reveals the names, he will die."

We looked up as Camila entered the interrogation room.

She placed her hands on Alexander and her golden aura radiated from her hand to his shoulder.

"Alexander, do you know who I am?"

He nodded, blood running down his face.

She wiped his eyes clean and grabbed the chair next to him.

"Look at me, my dear child." She delicately pulled his chin up so he could look into her eyes.

Her golden aura was glowing brighter now. Her eyes were as bright as the sun on a summer day.

"Alexander, who did this to you? Who has put a bind on you?"

He cried out, "I-I cannot say!"

Blood began dripping down from his ears now. His eyes were glowing a violent blue color.

I looked at my dad, who was pacing around the room. "Dad, he's going to die. Make them stop."

"I can't, Aria. The interrogations must go on. We have got to get it out of him."

My mom agreed with me, "Liam, they're going to end up killing him. You know that if there's a bind on him, we're not going to get any answers from him."

I stood up and started to walk towards the door. My dad shouted at me, "Aria, where are you going? What are you doing?"

"Someone has to stop this. He can't die." I stormed out of the room.

CHAPTER THIRTY-SIX

I walked into the room and Hunter tried to block me from interfering with Camila's interrogation.

"Aria, you can't be here. Go back to the observation room!"

"We can't keep doing this to him! He's going to die!"

Alexander's body began to shake violently and his eyes rolled to the back of his head.

Camila, standing over Alexander's body, raised her hands towards the sky. The Fae's body was lifted up and a bright, gold light was surrounding his now-limp body.

Camila shouted, "Aria, get the guys out of here. I need your help!"

Hunter and Jeffrey quickly left the room and I rushed to stand next to Camila. "What do you need me to do? Is he dead?"

"He's not dead ... yet. Put your hands on his head ..."

"Are you sure that's a good idea?"

"Aria, do it, quickly!"

I reached up and put my hands over his head. When I touched him, an electric shock ran through my body.

"What is this? Why am I getting electrocuted?"

Camila's eyes widened. "You can feel it?"

"Feel what?"

"The bind. The bind that was placed on him is torturing him from within."

My hands began to burn as the electric shocks grew stronger. "I guess I can feel it. They're getting stronger. It's hurting a little."

"Use your powers to find the source and destroy the bind. Concentrate and you'll be able to find it."

"I can't do it. I don't know how to reach into someone's mind."

"Aria, we're running out of time. Close your eyes and follow the electricity."

I closed my eyes as another surge of power ran through my body from Alexander's head. I kept my breath steady and waited for the next bolt.

A second later, it came to me like a dream. I saw a small orange flame that quickly grew brighter. I reached deep into his mind and slowly felt the shock running up my arm and into my body.

Camila's voice was a mumble now. "Aria, you can do this. Follow the bind and you'll find its core. When you're there, you'll use your energy to undo the bind."

I shouted, "It's hurting me. I don't know how much longer I can keep it up."

Alexander's body was limp but I could hear his voice inside of my head.

"Please, help me. It's here. It's killing me! I'll tell you whatever you need to know!"

I followed his voice, which made the electric spark grow brighter and then suddenly, I saw it.

There was a large orange ball of light that was twisted up like a ball of yarn.

I shouted out, "Camila, I see it. I see the core!"

"Good. Now Aria, I need you to channel all of your

energy towards it. You should be able to hold it. When you grab it, quickly begin to untie it. It's going to hurt but you can do it."

I squeezed my eyes closed tighter and felt myself running towards the electric mass.

I slowly started to put my hands over the mass and jumped back in surprise. Even though the mass was radiating with heat, it was ice-cold to my touch.

"Camila, it's cold, is there something wrong?"

"No, nothing wrong. That's perfect. Aria, get the bind untied before we lose him."

I took a deep breath and then slowly put my hands over the mass. The ice-cold feeling went through my entire body and I felt my body begin to change.

I looked down at my hands and saw that my body was shimmering in different specks of blue, green, and violet. I kept my concentration on untying the mass of orange flames.

What seemed like minutes later, the mass was untied and I let go of the flames.

As soon as I removed my hands from the flame, the bright flame extinguished.

I opened my eyes and Camila was staring at me,

with amazement in her eyes.

"Aria, you truly are special. You did it. You saved his life."

CHAPTER THIRTY-SEVEN

Hunter sent Jeffrey with the medics to make sure Alexander was healed and protected. My parents walked into the room together as I sat down next to Camila.

My mom walked over to me and wrapped her arms around me, a little too tightly. "Aria, what happened? How did you do that?"

I shrugged my shoulders and tried to get out from under her bear hug.

My dad must have seen me struggling, so he tried to get my mom off me too.

"Honey, let her breathe a bit."

My mom gave him an ugly stare as she pulled up the chair next to me.

"Liam, our daughter just reached into that man's mind. Are you not the least bit concerned as to what this all means?"

"Yes, that was a lot to process, but what I am more concerned with right now is that Alexander's bind is off, so we're going to be able to find out who the real traitors are."

Camila sat across from my mom and me.

"Liam, Adalyn, your daughter is not technically the Original Fae, but she is most definitely an Original."

My dad asked, "What exactly do you mean?"

Camila glanced me over and then put her hand on top of mine.

"Aria, when you've used your powers before, you have experienced your skin colors changing, correct?"

I nodded, "Yeah, I guess so."

"I think I know what it's called. Better yet, I think I know what you are called."

My mom chimed in, "With all due respect, we already know that, Camila. Aria is a Natural Elemental."

"Yes, you're right about that. She is a Natural."

My dad said, "Well, to be fair, she's a Natural who

isn't Light or Dark."

Camila nodded in agreement.

"Yes, she's the first of her kind. It all came to me during Alexander's unbinding though."

"I have a golden aura that surrounds me because of the power that is inside of me. Aria has something similar. There's a name for that kind of power."

My mom and dad stared at each other with confusion in their eyes.

Camila stood up and said, "Your daughter is the first of her kind, a Natural Fae with Elemancy."

CHAPTER THIRTY-EIGHT

My mom mumbled, "Elemancy?"

Camila nodded as my dad looked at me and her.

"What exactly do you mean she is a Fae with Elemancy?"

Camila gestured for me to place my other hand in hers. "Aria, when I call upon my powers to be used at great strengths, I start to radiate with my golden aura. My husband, Sebastian, also has this aura. Only his aura is extremely dark, almost like a blend of shadows."

Camila closed her eyes and I felt a warm tingling sensation run from her hands onto mine. I looked around us and saw that her body was glowing with her Elemancy light.

A second later, she opened her eyes. "Why don't you try to send me some of your energy?"

"I don't know that I can."

"Of course you can. You just unbound a Fae. You can do this."

My dad added, "I don't know if that's the best idea. In the past, when Aria's Elemancy came forth, she lost control. She was usually filled with some type of anger or fear."

I tried to defend myself, "Dad, when that happened at the Trebles', I didn't know who I was. I didn't know what I was going to choose. I've chosen myself. Let me try this."

He looked at my mom and she nodded. He stepped back as I closed my eyes. I felt a pulsing in my hand and focused sending the power through to Camila.

"Aria, open your eyes."

I slowly opened one eye, and then the other. My hand, arms, and entire body was radiating with different shades of blues, purples, and greens.

"It's beautiful, isn't it?" Camila whispered.

I felt a warm tear fall down my cheek. "I've always been so afraid of it. I thought when this happened it was because of the darkness in me."

Camila looked at me and then put her hands on my

cheek. "Even the Lightest Fae has some darkness in them. The difference between a completely rogue and Dark Fae and a Light is the ability to notice the darkness and use it wisely. We are the captains of our own ships."

I smiled and felt the warm tears drift from my cheeks towards my mouth. Camila removed her hands from my cheek and I looked down at my hands. The different colors were now reflecting like diamonds, and I felt a familiar warmth run through my entire body.

The electricity I felt when I first touched Grayson was now running through my body, and I felt it at the edge of my fingertips. I rubbed my fingers together and a bright light began to glow in my hand.

My mom seemed shocked. "Whoa. Aria, what are you doing?"

Camila looked at me with a smile on her face. "How does it feel?"

I continued to rub my fingers together and stared at my hands as the colors that reflected from my skin turned into a large ball of electricity. The ball was radiating blues, greens, and purples.

My dad, standing close to my mom, looked at me with awe in his eyes. "That is beautiful, Aria."

I took my eyes off the ball and saw that my parents, for the first time in a long time, were looking at me with pride in their eyes.

I began to squeeze the ball tightly and felt the electricity slowly begin to dissipate.

My body welcomed the energy. The warmth ran from my fingertips down to my toes.

I looked at Camila and then felt my eyes spark with excitement. "I think I know how to control this."

CHAPTER THIRTY-NINE

A couple of hours later, we finally made it back home. I was undressing and getting ready to put my pajamas on when my phone's text tone went off.

I grabbed a hair tie, put my hair up, and looked at my phone. It was Grayson.

"Hey. Are you all home? My parents are on their way there now. Two of our lead guards didn't show up for the interrogations today. Any luck on your side?"

I sat on the edge of my bed. "Yeah, well, kind of. One of our guys was bound and unable to say anything. I kind of unbound him and he's in recovery now. We'll get answers tomorrow morning, hopefully."

"You unbound him? How?"

"Long story. Lots happened. Why aren't you coming with your parents?"

"...."

"What is it? What's going on?"

"...Sorry, my parents want my brothers and me to stay here just in case those two guards show up. Andre is going with them, though."

"Alright, I'll text you when they leave here. Meet up for breakfast tomorrow?"

"Yeah, come over here. I'll cook you something."

"Yeah, I'll go over. No thanks to your cooking though. I'll bring something."

"Whatever. Hater."

"Ha ha. XOXO."

I set my phone down, got up, and walked towards my bedroom door.

"Alexia, can you come here?"

A few seconds later my sister was with me in my room.

"What's up?"

"Grayson's parents are on their way over here."

"Is everything alright? Have you told mom and dad?"

I shook my head, "Grayson said that two of their main guards didn't even show up for their interrogations."

"Shit. That makes them look a little guilty, don't you think?"

I nodded, "Yeah, but I wonder why the Trebles are coming over here."

"Maybe they just want to know what happened during our interviews."

"I don't know. It's just weird because Grayson isn't coming with them, I guess."

"Yeah, that's weird. We should probably go tell Mom and Dad they're on the way. Maybe we'll be able to stick around and be nosey."

I smiled at my sister, grabbed my robe, and followed her downstairs.

CHAPTER FORTY

My sister and I met my mom and dad in the kitchen, where they were talking to Hunter. I took the chair closest to Hunter and sat on it.

"Hey, what's going on?"

He looked at me and then at my parents. I could tell there was something he wasn't sure whether I should hear or not.

"I was just filling your parents in on Alexander's recovery."

I looked at my sister and gave her a warning stare.

"Oh yeah? What's new?"

My mom spoke before Hunter could, "Well, Alexander is going to be fully recovered overnight, hopefully. Camila is watching over him."

Hunter looked at Alexia and then at me. "Do either of you know anything about what happened at the Trebles'?"

My sister's face immediately turned red and she looked at me, begging for help.

"Uh, well, Grayson said his parents are on their way here. Apparently a couple of their main guards didn't even bother to show up to their interrogations this morning."

My dad looked at Hunter, "Don't you think it's odd that a couple of high-ranking Dark Fae guards didn't go to their mandatory interrogations, and now the head of the Dark Fae family are coming here unannounced?"

My mom chimed in, trying to sound positive, "Maybe they're just concerned and wanted to tell us in person?"

Hunter cleared his throat, "You said a couple of their main guards didn't show up? What about their head guard, Andre, I think his name is?"

"Andre passed his test. He's actually coming with Mr. and Mrs. Treble now."

Hunter looked relieved and then said, "I wonder if they've sent trackers after the two who didn't show up? Hopefully by tomorrow, we'll be able to get some sort of information out of Alexander."

As if on cue, Camila walked into the room. "Hello, everyone."

She walked towards me and then sat on the bar stool next to Alexia.

Hunter bowed his head in respect and then asked, "Do you think Alexander will be healthy enough to answer our questions tomorrow?"

Camila smiled and then nodded, "Yes, he's recovering quite well."

She turned back around and faced me. "Aria, you did a fantastic job unbinding him. For a Fae who's never done that, I'm surprised it really hasn't taken a toll on you. Are you feeling alright?"

I shrugged, "I haven't really thought about how I feel. I think I'm feeling fine."

I lifted my arms up and down. "I don't think anything hurts?"

She smiled at me. "Good, that's good. It's just that unbindings are so rare and powerful I wanted to make sure you're alright."

Alexia giggled, "She's the first of her kind, a true kick ass!"

I laughed as the doorbell rang. Hunter immediately started walking towards the door. "I'll get it, you all stay here."

My mom and dad stood up and gestured for us to join them. I looked at Camila, who stayed sitting down. "Aria, dear, can you get me the bottle of Chardonnay from the refrigerator? I feel like this is going to be a long night."

I smiled at her and then proceeded to get her the bottle and a wine glass. When I returned to the table, Mr. and Mrs. Treble were standing on the other side of the room with their security guard, Andre.

CHAPTER FORTY-ONE

Hunter broke the awkward silence as he walked back over towards my family. "Mr. and Mrs. Treble wanted to come and tell us what happened during their interrogations today. They felt like it could not wait."

My dad nodded, "Okay, well, welcome to our home. I hear that two of your head guards didn't show up for interrogations?"

Mr. Treble's jaw tightened. "You are correct. And I hear that Aria was able to unbind one of your guards who may have some information."

Mrs. Treble looked nervously at Andre and then at her husband. "What my husband isn't saying is that we were hoping your guard may give us some detail about the two guards who didn't come for their interrogations today."

Camila refilled her wine glass and then spoke before either of my parents could, "Alexander is not capable of speaking at the moment. He's still undergoing treatment. It may be days until he's able to even open his eyes."

Mr. Treble cleared his throat. "Of course, however, we do have Fae who can help him speak without taking too much energy, if needed."

I looked at my mom and dad, whose faces had turned red. I asked, "What do you mean you have Fae who can help him? He just needs rest."

Mr. Treble smiled at me. "We have Fae with unique powers to persuade one's mind to speaking to them."

My dad's voice sounded strained as he said, "You will not use those—those things on any of my Light Fae. And you will not bring them into our home!"

"What kind of Fae are you all talking about?" Alexia asked.

Camila mumbled, "It's the telepathic Fae. That power is unique to some very Dark Fae. There are not many with that capability."

Mr. Treble looked at his guard, Andre, with frustration in his eyes. Andre then looked at Hunter and then at me. "We have reason to believe that your relative, Violet, is the person collecting Fae and turning them against our houses."

Hunter asked, "Do you think that Violet's doing it for Sebastian?"

Andre shook his head, "No, we think she's actually doing this with her son."

I mumbled, "Ethan? You think that Ethan is actually helping her with this?"

Andre shook his head.

I looked at Camila, "Do you think I can help Alexander recover faster? We need answers."

My dad interrupted, "Absolutely not! Aria, you have done quite enough. You need to get rest yourself!"

My mom added, "Your dad's right. You've used a lot of energy already. I don't think it's safe for you to do anything else."

Camila stayed quiet and took slow sips of her wine.

I tugged on her arm. "Camila, what can I do to help speed up his recovery?"

Before she could answer, Andre's phone started to ring. He looked at it and then looked at us. "It's Cayne."

He answered, "Hello? ... Are you sure about that?

… Got dammit, are you sure it's them?… Alright, we're on our way back now."

He looked at the Trebles and then at my parents. "We should be going. Cayne says that Briar was outside working out and that when he was going back inside, a black SUV pulled up and dropped two bodies off on our front lawn."

Mrs. Treble gasped, "Is he okay?"

Andre nodded, "Yes, but it's our two guards. Their throats were slit. We should get back. Cayne and Briar were getting the bodies in the labs for us."

My dad stood up. "We will follow up with you all tomorrow if Alexander wakes up."

Mr. Treble nodded and grabbed his wife's hand as they followed Andre and Hunter out of the room.

CHAPTER FORTY-TWO

The next day I woke up a little past noon and felt like every bone in my body was aching. I shouted for my mom, "Mom, come here!"

A couple of seconds later my mom, looking flustered, walked into my room. "What is it? Are you alright?"

I forced myself to sit up and lean against the headboard. "I don't feel so good."

"Oh, Aria. We told you that you were overdoing it. Let me see..."

She put her hand on my forehead to check for a temperature and I felt her ice-cold hand against my skin as soon as she made contact with my head.

My mom pulled her hand away as quickly as she placed it on my head. "Oh my goodness, Aria, you're burning up! Let me go and get the doctor.

You haven't had a fever like this since you were a baby!"

As my mom left the room, I threw my blankets off of me and forced myself to walk across the room so I could get some water and my cell phone. I started drinking the water and glanced at my phone.

Crap. Eleven missed calls, three voicemails, and eight text messages.

I slowly started to make my way back to my bed when Camila, my mom, and our doctor walked into my room.

My mom shouted, "Aria! Get back in bed. You really should not be walking right now."

Camila and the doctor walked towards me and helped me get settled back into bed.

Dr. Brushwick is a dark skinned, bald man who has been the doctor for the head Light Fae families for as long as anyone could remember.

He took my temperature and immediately began to hook me up to an IV.

"Is she going to be okay? What's wrong with her?" My mom was now pacing around the room.

The doctor stayed quiet as Camila responded,

"Aria's going to be just fine. She just overdid it yesterday. She's basically just dehydrated. Am I right, Dr. Brushwick?"

He looked at her and then at my mom. "That's right—just need to get some liquids in her and she'll be just fine."

I looked at my phone again. "Mom, have you heard from the Trebles?"

She looked at me and took a seat at the edge of my bed. "Yes, we have. They'll be over for dinner tonight. We are having a meeting because it looks like your aunt and cousin are the ones who slit the throats of two Dark Fae guards."

"Is Grayson coming with them?"

She nodded, "The entire family will be here."

I began to look at some of my texts and saw that they were mainly from Grayson, confirming everything my mom just said.

Camila walked Dr. Brushwick out of the room and then, before leaving the room with him, turned around and said, "Aria, Alexander has woken up. He's ready to cooperate with us whenever we're ready. Thank you for all that you did to unbind him."

I smiled and nodded, "That's great. I'd like to be

there for his interrogation, so if that could wait until tomorrow or something ..."

She returned my smile. "Of course. We can wait until you've recovered."

A second later she was gone, and my sister joined my mom and me in my room.

"Wow, you look like crap."

I threw a pillow at her. "Yeah, I feel like it."

She laughed. "Anyways, Mom, did you tell Aria that the Trebles are coming over?"

"Yes, I did."

"Did you tell her about Ethan and Violet?"

My mom's face turned red and she glared at my sister. "Yes, I told her about their roles with the Dark Fae's deaths."

My sister looked confused. "But what about—?"

My mom cut her off. "One thing at a time, Alexia. Aria will be caught up at dinner tonight. Why don't you get out of here so your sister can get some rest before our guests arrive."

Alexia walked out of the room and my mom turned back to face me. "Alright sweetie, why don't you get some sleep and I'll wake you up an hour before dinner so you have time to get your-self together a bit? I know you wouldn't dare miss out on a meeting, so I'm not going to even try and fight you on this."

I smiled at her. "Thanks, Mom. Love you."

CHAPTER FORTY-THREE

I slept for what felt like days and woke up to my mom's soft, cold hands. "Aria, baby, how are you feeling?"

I slowly sat up. "Can you get me some water?" My voice was cracking and as my mom walked across the room to get me water, I moved my arms and legs and noticed they weren't hurting as bad as earlier.

I drank the water and smiled at my mom. "I feel a little better. My body isn't hurting."

She put her hand on my forehead, "You're still a bit warm, but you do look better. Maybe your body just needed a day of rest."

I looked down at my arm and asked, "Where's my IV?"

"Dr. Brushwick took it out about an hour ago. We decided to let you sleep a little longer."

I looked at my cell phone. "What time are the Trebles going to be here?"

My mom sighed, "They'll be here in about an hour. Are you sure you don't want to get more rest tonight? I promise to update you on our meeting."

I shook my head, "If it has anything to do with Violet and Ethan, I need to be there."

My mom nodded, "Alright, well, if you want to start getting ready, I've got a dress laid out for you. This will be a formal dinner, as the entire Dark Royal family will be here."

I looked over at my make-up vanity and saw a white gown with gold stripes hanging next to it.

I pointed, "Is that the dress I'm wearing tonight?"

My mom smiled, "Yeah, it's pretty, isn't it? Your sister helped me pick it out. I'll see you downstairs."

She turned away and slowly walked out of my room.

I grabbed my cell and texted Grayson:
> *Sorry I've been sick, in bed all day. I'm feeling a bit better now. I'll see*
> *you in a while ;)*

A few seconds later he replied:

Alexia texted me earlier. Glad you're feeling better. Lots to talk about

tonight. See you soon."

I got up and showered and as I was getting dressed, my sister knocked on my door. "Hey, are you naked or can I come in?"

I laughed, "Come in."

She walked in with a long white gown with silver beads dripping from the top.

"I love the silver on your dress, Alexia."

She tugged at it. "Yeah this is so pretty, I just don't understand why we're having to get so dressed up for this dinner. It's a bit weird."

My sister pointed at my dress and I looked down and saw that strings of gold beads were flowing under the white veil looking material. "It's a little much, huh?"

"Yeah, I guess. Your dress is gorgeous, Aria."

I looked at it in the mirror and then stared at my messy hair. "Will you help me with my hair? I just don't have the energy, to be honest."

She laughed, "Alright, sit down."

I sat at the vanity and she started to get my hair together. "Are you nervous to see Grayson in such a formal setting?"

I shrugged, "Not really. It's just a meeting and dinner."

"Our parents are the head Light Fae, and his family are the Dark Royals. This could be good or bad."

"I think everyone should focus on Violet and Ethan right now. They're kind of the mutual enemy, don't you think?"

"Yeah, I just think that everyone's going to blame each other for all of this."

I smiled and sprayed hairspray on my hair. "I think it's going to be just fine."

A couple of seconds later, the doorbell rang.

My sister and I looked at each other. I smiled at her, "I guess this is it, huh?"

She looked at me and started walking out of my room. "Yeah, I guess so. I just need to sit by you because I don't like when dad gets all mad and I'm near him."

I laughed and followed her downstairs.

CHAPTER FORTY-FOUR

I walked into the dining room and saw the Trebles standing around, mumbling to each other.

I greeted them, "Hi, Mr. and Mrs. Treble, it's good to see you two again."

They both embraced me with a half-hug. Mrs. Treble smiled, "You look rested, I heard you weren't feeling good today."

"Yeah, I was dehydrated and slept almost all day. I feel better now, though."

"That's good."

I walked over towards Cayne, Briar, and Grayson to greet them. "Hey guys. Have my parents been in here yet?"

Grayson held my hand and our normal spark was a little weaker than usual tonight. I looked down at our hands and he lifted my head up with his free hand. "Your parents are finalizing things. Hunter greeted us, though."

Cayne asked, "Have you all been able to talk to the Fae who you unbound?"

I shook my head.

Before I could say anything, my mom walked into the room. "Hello, everyone. Please, follow me to the dining area."

We all walked through the hallway and saw that there were name cards on the table. I looked over at Alexia, who was standing a couple of feet behind me.

I whispered, "There's assigned seating…"

She took a closer look. "Got dammit. You've got to be kidding me."

We walked towards the table and I saw that I was sitting between Camila and Grayson.

Alexia found her card and saw that she was sitting across from me, but between my mom and Cayne. I whispered, "At least you're not sitting next to dad."

My dad cleared his throat as he stood at the head of the table. "Why wouldn't you want to sit next to me, Alexia?"

My sister's face turned red and we started to giggle as my dad looked at the both of us with disapproving eyes. We immediately got quiet as everyone took their seats.

Mr. Treble stood at the end of the table, across from my dad. Andre, the Dark Fae head guard, stood by his side, while Hunter stood by my dad's side.

My dad signaled for everyone to take their seats. "Thank you all for joining us tonight. I'd like for everyone to know that this meeting is being recorded and is on the record for both parties."

I looked at Grayson, confused. I mumbled, "Why is this so formal?"

He shrugged as his dad spoke. "Thank you for having us over on a more formal notice this time. Shall we get started?"

My dad nodded, "Dinner will be served as we meet. If anyone has special requests, please just ask one of our servers for help."

Mr. Treble smiled and then started, "Last night we left here because our two guards who had been missing were dropped off with their throats slit. We ran numerous tests through the night and have confirmed that Violet and Ethan Whitelace were the Fae responsible for this."

My mom asked, "How did you all come to this conclusion? How were the bodies so easily dropped off on your lawn?"

Cayne answered, "We ran tests and found traces of their imprints on both of their bodies."

Braden added, "And as for the bodies, most of our guards were off for the evening because they were all on duty during the day for interrogations."

I asked, "Do you think that Violet and Sebastian knew you wouldn't have guards last night?"

I felt Grayson stare at me as his dad answered me. "We believe they have someone inside of our house working for them. That is why we are meeting here, and not at our home."

Camila spoke for the first time, "What are you all going to do to figure out who it is? Did everyone participate in the interrogations?"

Mrs. Treble nodded, "Yes, everyone except the two dead guards took and passed our interrogations."

I was confused so I had to ask, "How would they pass all of your interrogations if they are still helping Violet and Ethan?"

Mr. Treble looked at me and then at my dad. He

cleared his throat, "Well, this brings us to another thing I'd like to talk with your family about. We were hoping you'd be able to be a part of our interrogations."

"You need my help?" I asked.

Grayson spoke now, "With Violet working with Sebastian, we feel like they may have figured out a way around our interrogation. Our interrogations, like yours, began centuries ago. We think Sebastian told Violet about some possible loopholes."

I mumbled, "Wow."

My dad's voice rose an octave, "I don't think it's smart for Aria to help. Aria, look how much energy this took out of you. I don't think you could do it again. At least not so soon."

My mom added, "Aria, you're still not a hundred percent recovered and healed. It's not smart."

Mrs. Treble took a sip of her tea and then spoke, "Aria, I understand you're not feeling well, we were just hoping sometime in the next few days, when you are feeling better, you'll be able to help us with a surprise round of interrogations."

"If I did it, I don't know that I could unbind someone again. I did it, it hurt, and Camila helped me with it."

Cayne was speaking now, "We don't think any of our guards would actually be bound. I don't think Violet would place a bind on any of our guards because she won't expect us to have figured all of this out, at least not so soon."

My dad was about to say something until I cut him off, "I'll do it. I'll need a few days, but I'll do it. What exactly is the plan?"

My mom and dad were going to protest until Alexia said, "Let's hear them out."

Andre spoke for the first time since arriving, "We would host interrogations on one day, at random. The guards will be told that we're all having our monthly training sessions, and on that day, we'd have you join me during our interrogations."

Hunter, who had been whispering in my dad's ear a second ago, butted in, "I don't think it'd be smart for Aria to be alone with all of your Dark Fae."

Andre leaned down and said something to Mr. Treble, whose head nodded a couple of seconds later.

He stood back up. "We would be more than happy to have you join her, and if Camila felt like she needed to attend, we could make accommodations for that as well."

Camila smiled, "Thank you. I am pretty sure I'd be okay on my own, but I do like the fact that Hunter would be in the room with Aria, you know, a little reassurance."

Andre nodded.

My dad's voice came out with a strong bass, "We should be there as well. Aria is our daughter, after all."

Grayson looked at me nervously and then spoke before anyone else did, "With all due respect, Mr. Whitelace, we don't think that would be the best thing for Aria."

My mom responded to Grayson before my dad could, "And why exactly would her parents being there not be a good idea?"

Cayne added, "We feel that Aria would be distracted if any of your family was there. I also personally believe that she'll be able to accomplish what we need rather easy. Her powers are extremely unique."

"Well, of course her powers are unique. She's the first and only of her kind," Camila interrupted.

Cayne continued, "Camila, please, you'll be more than welcome to be there with her. We just don't think Aria will be able to keep a clear mind if her family members are there."

"I'll go alone. I don't need anyone there!" I shouted in frustration.

My parents were about to protest when Alexia came to my defense, "I don't think Aria needs any of us there. Cayne's right. We'll just be a distraction, and she'll need all of her energy to focus during the interrogations."

I agreed, "Yeah, and I wouldn't be doing any unbinding."

After a couple of awkward seconds, my dad spoke up, "Very well then. Aria, you may go to the Trebles' after another day of rest. Camila and Hunter must be with you, though."

I felt a smile spread across my face as I reached back for Grayson's hand underneath the table, and as his skin touched mine, there were literal sparks that lit up.

Everyone looked at us and we blushed as Mr. Treble spoke, "Liam, I promise that Aria will be safe in our home. Hunter will be allowed in the interrogation room and Camila will be in the viewing room with us. I think she might be able to detect anything weird from there."

Camila nodded.

Cherise went on, "We know that Aria is your life. We feel the same way about our kids. That is why we need her help to find the traitors."

Our servers walked into the room with trays of food, and the room was suddenly quiet again.

As we began to eat, Camila asked, "Aria, have the sparks between you and Grayson changed since you declared yourself?"

I almost choked on my chicken and reached for my drink as I cleared my throat. I felt my face turn red. "What do you mean?"

"Well, we all saw and felt the sparks when you touched hands a few moments ago, and I was wondering if it's changed since you declared that you're not going Light or Dark?"

"Um, I don't think it's changed that much. Why?

"It's just the Destructive Fire works for Light and Dark who are not supposed to be together. So I wonder, why does it still show signs of existing in you two if you are neither Light nor Dark?"

Grayson chimed in, "Do you think the three of us could talk about this in private?"

We look around and saw that his parents and mine were listening to us very closely.

Camila smiled, "Sure, why don't the two of you come up to my room after dinner?"

We nodded and then continued to eat our dinner in silence.

CHAPTER
FORTY-FIVE

After the rest of our awkward dinner, Grayson and I broke away from our families to join Camila in her room.

We walked in and saw her sitting at the large, white piano in the corner of her room.

Grayson asked, "Do you play?"

She turned around and smiled. "Oh, no. I used to, but that was another lifetime ago."

As if she were stuck in a daydream, she physically shook her head. "Well, why don't you two sit?"

She pointed at two golden chairs that were a couple of feet away from her. We sat down awkwardly while she pulled her piano bench closer to us.

"I know that you both know what the Destructive Fire is."

We nodded.

"But like I was saying at dinner, I figured because you didn't choose the Light or the Dark, it'd be gone."

I shrugged, "I haven't really thought about it really."

She smiled, "Think about it or not, it's obviously still burning between the two of you, and that's a dangerous thing. It can quickly turn your love into a sick, sick hate. Ask my ex-husband."

Grayson, sounding a little irritated, mumbled, "We're not you."

I pushed his knee. "Grayson!"

Camila's smile was stuck on her face still. "Let him say what he needs to. He's right, you all are not him and I. But I say all of this because I don't want either of you to have hatred in your heart like he does. The fire can destroy both of you but boomerang more darkness onto one of you."

"Aria and I love each other. We'd never be able to hate each other."

"What if you all had to choose between each other or one of your relatives?"

I spoke before Grayson could, "That would never happen."

Camila let out a long sigh, "Never say never, Aria."

I looked at Grayson and then stood up in frustration. "So what do you suggest we do? What can we do to fix it?"

Camila reached for her glass of water, took a drink, and then turned back to look at me. "I don't know really. This has never happened. I did have an idea, though."

Grayson asked, "And that is?"

"I was thinking, when we go to your family's house in a couple of days, I could browse through your libraries. There's a book that I think you all have that may have some answers."

Grayson looked at her and then at me, confused. "A book? Why don't you ask Cayne? He's familiar with our family's library. I'm sure he could get you the book."

She shook her head. "The book will only show itself to an Original. And the last Original to have it was my ex-husband. He would have placed it in the Dark Fae's royal library."

"So I'll be with Hunter during the interrogations.

How will you get away from Mr. and Mrs. Treble?"

"I was hoping Grayson could help me with this part."

His eyebrows went up in surprise. "What do you need me to do?"

"I'll need you to distract your family during the interrogations so I can break away. It won't take me long. If the book is there, like I think it is, I'll be able to find it very quickly."

He nodded, "Okay. I'm in, Aria, what about you?"

I sighed, "Yeah, I'm in. Whatever helps us with this damn fire. It can't happen to us."

Camila smiled, "Very well then. I better get ready for bed. Thank you both for joining me."

We stood and up and walked back downstairs to join our families.

As Grayson and I walked downstairs, we held hands and felt the burning sensation run through our bodies.

We joined our families in the living area and Mrs. Treble smiled at us as we took a seat next to her. "Is everything alright?"

We nodded and then Mr. Treble stood up. "Why

don't we head home? It's getting late, and Aria, you need to get more rest."

Everyone followed suit and stood up and said their goodbyes.

CHAPTER FORTY-SIX

The next day, I stayed lounging in bed until noon and then walked downstairs. I walked into the kitchen and noticed that everyone was gone. I got my cell phone and called my mom, only to get her voicemail.

I grabbed orange juice and then texted Alexia:
Where are you? Where is everyone?

I had started to put butter on a bagel when my phone went off. It was Alexia. "Hello?"

"Hey, we're at the school. There was another incident. We're on our way back home now."

"What? Is everyone okay?"

"Thankfully, yes. But there were a number of Fae who tried breaking in last night, but guards were able to get rid of them."

"Wow, um. Okay. I'll see you all soon."

I hung up the phone and then texted Grayson:

> *Hey. Did you hear about what happened at the school last night?*

A few seconds later, he responded:

> *Yeah, that's insane. I heard that it was a group of Light and Dark Fae*
>
> *that were trying to break in.*

I took a bite of my bagel.

> *What the hell? Alexia didn't tell me that.*

> *Yeah, it's crazy. How are you feeling?*

> *I'm alright. Just having brunch. Going to lay in bed and watch movies all day. I'll see you tomorrow?*

> *Sounds good. XOXO*

I sent him the kissing emoji face and then headed back up to my room.

As I got to the top of the stairs, my stomach started to burn. I felt my fingers start to tingle with a fiery sensation. I looked around and took a deep breath. There were Dark Fae in my house. A lot of them.

I felt my skin and eye sockets begin to burn as my skin turned to shades of blue and purple. As I looked at a hallway mirror, I saw my eyes were burning a bright golden color that reminded me a lot of Camila's.

I clicked my fingers together and a deep purple flame was now in my palm. I shouted, "Come out of hiding, you cowards! I know you're here!"

Two men with purple eyes appeared in the hallway.

The man on the left smiled. His teeth looked like razor blades.

"What do you want? Why are you here?"

The man on the right, who was holding a purple flame in his hand, chuckled, "We're here for you, silly."

I threw my flame at him and then clapped my hands together as a burst of wind came through the hallway. I pushed the wind towards the men, and the man with razored teeth jumped to the ceiling and then crawled towards me.

The man who was holding the flame was immediately knocked down by my wind.

I looked at him with disgust, "What are you?"

The other man, who was hanging just above me now, dropped down and tilted his head as he ran one of his bony fingers through my hair. "We are the new Fae. The Fae without limits."

I laughed as I reached for his throat. Instead of being scared, his mischievous smile somehow stayed on his face. I let fire run from the inside of my chest through my arm, then into my hand and onto his skin.

His body began to shake violently before erupting into a pile of goo that quickly smelled like dead body.

I walked towards the man who was lying on the floor and then heard a noise come from one of the rooms to my right.

I closed my eyes and rubbed my hands together. Suddenly, four rings of fire similar to handcuffs were in my hands. I put one on each hand and leg of the Fae that was on the ground and walked over to the room.

I slowly entered the room and as soon as I walked in, the door slammed shut behind me. I felt my eyes burning extremely bright to make up for the lack of light in the room.

I shouted, "Come out! What do you want?"

Chills ran down my neck and then quickly down my back when I heard *his* voice.

I turned around to see my cousin—Ethan. Or at

least I thought it was him.

The thing that's standing between the door and me resembles my cousin, except his teeth match the other Fae. They're razor sharp. His eyes are still glowing a bright purple, but the core of his eyes are as black as night.

He tilted his head and took a step towards me. "Hello, cousin."

I immediately took a step backwards and snapped my fingers, summoning a ball of electric fire.

"What are you doing here? What happened to you?"

He smiled and made a strange clicking sound with his tongue. "I came for you. Don't you see? Mother has made me stronger."

I took another step back. "That's impossible. And how'd you get in here?"

His smile grew larger and more animated. "Not every Light Fae is working for your family."

"Oh, we know. We caught him."

My cousin looked confused. "You caught him? Really? How could that be possible if we were able to get in just now?"

"We got Alexander."

Ethan let out a laugh that sounded like a grunt.

"Oh, my dear cousin. Mom was right about you. You are so naive."

I lifted my palm up and sent a bolt of fire towards him.

My cousin jumped back and dodged my attack. He snapped his finger and a purple flame appeared between his fingertips. "You're not the only one who has all of these new tricks."

He attacked me and I lifted up a clear veil that blocked the flame.

He started walking back towards me and as he reached my defensive veil, he pointed a finger with a long, sharp nail at me. His eyes turned a notch brighter and then his nail glowed purple. He suddenly began to rip my veil with his fingernail.

I immediately turned around to run downstairs, and as I got to the edge of the top stair, my family walked in and Hunter was suddenly at my side.

"Aria, are you alright? What's going on?"

His eyes burned a bright blue and then looked back at my parents, shocked. "There are Dark Fae here. Stay there."

I felt myself shaking with anger. Hunter and Camila were tugging at my sleeves.

I looked up and into Camila's golden eyes.

She looked back at me and I saw worry in her eyes. "Aria, what is in here?"

I mumbled, "It's Ethan. But he's different."

Hunter asked, "What do you mean he's different?"

"I mean he has more powers, he's stronger. He doesn't look normal."

We walked back towards the room we had just been in and just as we were turning the light on, Ethan and three other Fae jumped out the window.

Camila let out a long sigh. "My ex-husband once tried to build an army of Dark Fae, and rumors were that they were practicing mixing Light and Dark powers. Those things. They looked just like his creations."

Hunter asked, "Are there any notes on these things in that book that Aria told me about? You know, the one you're going to be looking for at the Dark Royals?"

Camila nodded, "I think so. But Sebastian never truly succeeded in creating the perfect Fae because eventually, all of them died out from turning against each other."

I shook my head, still in shock, "Ethan said his mom did it to him, not Sebastian."

Camila walked towards the window where Ethan had jumped and rubbed her hand against the windowsill. She lifted her hand and there was a black, oil-like substance.

"If my ex-husband didn't do this, I don't see how Violet would be able to."

Hunter walked closer to Camila and touched the oily substance as well.

"Is this blood?"

Camila nodded, "Why don't you take samples to our labs? We can look at them after we talk to Alexander."

I asked, "Is he well enough to talk?"

Hunter nodded now, "Yes, he's fully recovered and is being guarded in a high-security room."

"Alright, I guess we should go get Mom and Dad caught up with what happened?"

Camila wiped her hands clean. "Why don't you let me get them caught up while you shower and get ready for Alexander's interrogation?"

Hunter added, "That sounds like a good idea. And I'll get this all cleaned up."

I nodded and headed towards my room.

CHAPTER FORTY-SEVEN

As I entered my room I grabbed my phone to text Grayson:

> *Ethan broke into my house a while ago. I'm fine. Everyone here is fine. I'll call you later. I'm about to start Alexander's interrogations in a bit.*

He quickly texted back:

> *Ethan? Are you serious? Call me ASAP.*

> *I will as soon as I'm done with Alexander.*

> *Okay. Ttyl.*

I put my phone on the counter and went to start a bath.

As my bath was warming, I stared at myself in the mirror. I looked at my eyes and saw that there was something floating in them. I got closer to the mirror to see if it was an eye lash or something, but it wasn't. It looked like golden flakes were floating in my eyes.

I put my hand on my right eye, and the left eye glowed a light gold as if it were refocusing.

I went back and forth, from eye to eye, before I noticed that my mirror was fogging up from the hot bath.

I turned off the bath water and chose to take a quick shower instead.

A few moments later, someone was knocking on my bathroom door.

"Hey, Aria. Are you alright? I heard what happened." It was Alexia.

I grabbed my robe and wrapped it around me. "Yeah, come in."

She walked in and sat on the bench near the door.

"How long have you been in here? It's so hot." She re-opened the bathroom door to let some of the steam out.

"Sorry, I was going to take a hot bath but decided to just shower instead."

My sister looked at me and then at the floor. "Are you sure you're okay?"

Alexia got up and walked towards me. I took a step back, not wanting her to see my eyes, but it was too late. Almost as if she had read my mind, she grabbed onto my arm tightly.

"Aria, what's going on with your eyes? Why are they gold?"

I felt myself blush and then felt my eyes begin to shine bright.

"I-I don't know. I just saw them when I was getting my bath ready. I thought I had something in my eye, but I looked closer and … yeah."

My sister stepped closer to me. "Let me see."

She was now in my personal space and held my left eye open with two of her fingers.

"Your eyes literally have gold pieces floating in them. How is that possible? We should call Mom and—"

I cut her off, "No. I don't want to bring it up if I don't have to."

"Let's be real, you think they're not going to notice?"

I shrugged, "Do you think I should tell Camila before Mom and Dad?"

My sister thought for a second. "Maybe. Maybe she'll know what they are."

I took a deep breath, "Screw it. I'm going to show all of them. If something's wrong with me, Mom and Dad should know, and Camila may be able to help out."

My sister nodded in agreement, "Alright, I'll get everyone together downstairs. This should be good."

I let out a stressed laugh and threw a towel at her. "See you in a few."

CHAPTER FORTY-EIGHT

I got dressed as quickly as I could and headed downstairs to tell—or rather, to show—everyone what was happening to me now.

When I got downstairs my mom was looking me up and down. "Is everything okay, Aria? Alexia said you needed to talk to us?"

I glared at my sister. Couldn't she have been a bit more discreet or said she wanted a family meeting or something?

"I think I'm fine … I mean, I feel fine."

Camila was standing across the room with her arms crossed. "Are you ready to talk with Alexander now?"

I nodded and before I could take a step, my mom stopped me. "Wait a second."

She walked towards me and then grabbed my face,

mumbling, "What in the world ..."

I didn't notice that my dad wasn't in the room until he walked in with Hunter by his side. "What's going on here?"

My mom's eyes were glowing a bright blue, filled with worry. "Oh, Aria. What is happening to you?"

Camila was quickly by my side now. "Let me see ..."

She was holding onto my face when her eyes began to radiate their usual golden aura.

"Aria, right when I think I've got you figured out, you show up with another surprise ..."

My dad asked, "What is it?"

Hunter quickly interjected, "I'm going to get things ready with Alexander. I'll meet you all in the interrogation rooms."

My dad nodded as he continued his walk towards my mom, Camila, and me.

Camila spoke first, "It seems that Aria's powers have just grown. Taking on all of those Fae; it must have sparked something in you. Something that was sitting dormant and waiting for the right time to be released."

My mom asked, "What does this mean?"

Camila finally let go of my face. "It means nothing at all. Aria is just fine. She's just going to become a lot stronger. We all knew she was an Original Fae for her kind, consider this just the cherry on top."

My mom and dad let out a sigh of relief.

After a couple of seconds, my dad cleared his throat, "Well then, let's get to Hunter and Alexander."

We all left the room, my sister and me trailing a few feet behind everyone else.

She whispered, "This should be interesting, huh?"

I nodded and slowly followed everyone towards the interrogation rooms.

As we got closer to the rooms, I felt my chest burn. I don't know if it was from my nerves, anxiety or what, but it was definitely strange.

Alexia pulled on my arm, "What is it? Are you alright?"

I shrugged, unsure as to what to tell her.

"Camila said you're going to be just fine, don't worry about it."

"I'm not worried about myself. I'm just not sure I'm ready to hear what Alexander has to say during the interrogations."

My sister let out a quiet laugh, "Oh I'm ready. I'm ready to find out who the damn traitors are and get them all out of here and away from the Trebles as well."

I let out a long sigh, "Yeah, I guess you're right."

We finally made it to the interrogation rooms and when we walked in, Alexander, who was sitting in front of Hunter, immediately stood up.

He addressed my dad, "Mr. Whitelace, you have to believe me. I didn't want to do anything they asked. I was forced to."

My dad looked at Hunter and then at Camila. "We'll see about that."

CHAPTER FORTY-NINE

We all sat behind Hunter as he asked Alexander to sit back down. As I took my seat, I felt Alexander's eyes focusing on me. I looked up and as soon as I made eye contact with him, he began to cry.

"You! You saved my life! Thank you so much, Ms. Whitelace!"

Camila spoke to him before I could respond, "Do you know why she saved your life, Alexander?"

He shook his head.

"We need you to tell us who the traitors are. Aria was attacked earlier and before it happens again, we need to know who is responsible."

Alexander's attention was on me immediately. "They're not going to stop coming. They're going to keep on until they get what they want."

My dad shouted, "Who are they? What do they

want?"

Alexander looked around at all of us with confusion in his eyes. He laughed with disbelief, "You all really don't know?"

"Know what?" I asked.

"There are so many of them. So many of the Light Fae who are joining Sebastian and Violet."

"Why are they joining them? What would make them want to do that?"

He looked around and then pointed at Camila. "Because of her. Because of Sebastian."

Camila huffed with clear frustration, "What exactly are you talking about?"

He tried to stand up but Hunter quickly pushed him back down.

"Answer their questions, Alexander."

"They don't want to hide from the humans anymore. They want to be free to live with their powers in the mundane world. Violet is promising them that kind of future."

I laughed, "A future where they look and become like monsters? My cousin doesn't even look like himself anymore. Those things I saw, they weren't

Fae. They were hideous … things."

"They weren't Light Fae … those were Dark Fae who volunteered to be turned. The Light Fae are sharing their powers with Violet and Sebastian and then are being watched over by the New Order."

Camila stood up, "What did you just say?"

Alexander smiled, "I thought that might catch your attention. The New Order. Sebastian has brought them back."

My parents looked at each other confused and then my dad asked, "Who is the New Order, Camila?"

She looked back at us and then mumbled, "It's not really who they are, but what they are."

Camila put her hand on Alexander. "Are you joining them?"

Alexander shook his head violently, "No, no, never. I have pledged my loyalty to the Light Fae Family."

Camila's eyes glowed their bright golden color. "Do not lie to me, boy."

She placed her long finger on the center of his forehead and then closed her eyes.

Alexander began to shake and then shouted out, "Please, stop!"

A second later, Camila removed her finger from his head and Alexander's eyes were wide open.

"Ho-how did you do that?"

"Did you forget that I am the Original Light Fae? I had to see if you were lying."

The room was quiet for an awkward second until Alexia asked, "So, was he lying? Is he one of theirs?"

Camila shook her head, "I don't think we'll need to worry about Alexander betraying this family again. However, I don't think we can fully trust him with his old duties again. He's too easy to manipulate."

Alexander pleaded, "Mr. Whitelace, I beg you, give me another chance."

My dad stood up and then looked at Hunter. "Take him to the cellars. Get the list of names of all those compromised. And then release Mr. Bitton of his duties."

"Sir, please, I don't have anywhere to go."

Hunter cleared his throat, "That is not our problem anymore."

My mom and dad exited the room, Camila a couple of seconds after. I stuck around with my sister for a few moments longer.

"What did Camila do to you?"

Alexander looked up at me with tears in his eyes. "She read my memories and my thoughts. I couldn't hide anything from her."

Alexia wrapped her arms around herself. "That's really weird," she whispered.

I asked Hunter, "What are we going to do? Are we just going to fire all of our guards?"

Hunter sighed, "I don't know. I'm hoping there's not that many people involved."

Alexander laughed, "There are so many of them. You all have no idea. Violet's promise is just too good for anyone to pass up. That's why Fae from both sides are jumping ship. She's basically promising them the world."

Hunter glared at Alexander and then said, "Do they all actually think that Violet is going to just let them live on their own free will?"

Alex nodded.

I added, "They can't all be that naive."

"Well, it seems like they are. Violet's promise is that Fae will be the leading species on Earth and the humans will be our subordinates. Think about the things we could accomplish with our powers."

Hunter let out a sound that was similar to a grunt. "The humans will never let that happen. We live under the radar for not only the safety of the mundanes, but for our sake, too."

I looked down at my phone and saw missed calls from Grayson. I looked back up. "Hunter, let's get out of here. We can come back later."

Hunter nodded and Alexander started to whimper, "Wha-what about me?"

We both turned to face him. "You don't have anywhere to go, right?" I asked.

Hunter smiled at me and we headed out of the interrogation rooms.

CHAPTER FIFTY

As I was walking back towards my room, Alexia shouted out, "Aria, get over here! Quick!"

I walked into the living area and saw that she was standing with my mom looking at her phone screen.

"What's going on?"

My mom looked at me and then handed me the phone.

I grabbed it from her and felt her hands shaking. I looked down at the phone and saw the Trebles' house.

"What is this?"

"Just watch …" my mom said.

A second later, the Trebles' home went up in flames.

I cried out, "Oh my God!"

I immediately reached for my phone and dialed Grayson's number.

He answered after half a ring, "Hello Ar—?"

I cut him off, "Are you okay? Is your family okay? Wha-what happened?"

"Calm down. We're all okay. It was Violet. She just staged a coup."

"What do you mean?"

"A bunch of our most trusted guards have turned against us and joined them. I don't know what they're being promised, but I can't believe it. Everything we had just went up in flames."

"Where are you all going?"

There was no response for a couple of seconds.

"Grayson? Where are you all going?"

"I-I don't know. I think some warehouse. But Andre isn't even sure that it's safe there anymore."

I looked around at my family, who were all staring at me, and then said, "Why don't you all come over here? You know it's safe here."

My mom and dad looked at me with a mixture of confusion and anger in their eyes.

I turned around and saw Camila smiling and nodding her head in agreement with me.

I heard Grayson talking to someone in the background and then he said, "Alright, we'll be on our way soon. We're just going to stop by the safe house and pick up a few things."

"Okay, I'll see you soon. Please, be careful."

Grayson hung up and then I immediately turned around to tell everyone what was going on.

"There was a coup at the Dark Royals' house. They've lost everything. Even some of their most trusted guards have joined Violet."

"Well I guess we should get the guest level prepared for them then, huh?" My mom asked with a little annoyance in her voice.

"I know it's a little weird to have the Dark Royal family here, but what else are we supposed to do? Let them risk their lives by staying at their supposed 'safe house'?"

My dad finally spoke up, "It isn't weird that you're inviting your boyfriend's family here after they've lost everything. However, it is weird that his family just happens to be the Dark Royals. Our ancestors will probably be turning in their graves when we just let the Dark Fae walk in and sleep here."

Camila's soft, calm voice broke through my dad's frustration, "I think our ancestors would understand that we're doing the right thing. Plus, the Dark Fae are nothing like they used to be. We are not at war with the Dark Fae, and correct me if I'm wrong, but we haven't had a war in a very long time."

My dad added, "Yes, that is because we have strict laws forbidding interaction between us and them. When you start to mingle with darkness, things like ... like this happen." He was pointing at the phone which had a still image of the Trebles' house in flames.

"Maybe we'll be stronger against Violet and Sebastian together, rather than apart," my sister, whom I had forgotten was in the room, said.

"We will have a meeting in the council chambers with our guests as soon as they get settled in. All members of both families will need to be in attendance." My dad looked at Hunter, "You'll need to be there as well. You're one of the few guards we can trust."

Hunter nodded and then we all headed our separate ways.

CHAPTER FIFTY-ONE

Grayson and his family finally arrived, after what felt like forever. I showed them our guest level, which was just above the basements, and assured them that our home was their home, even if it were just for the time being. As I was showing Briar and Cayne their room, Hunter's voice came over the intercom system.

"Attention everyone: Please make your way to the main level for an immediate meeting. Again, everyone, please come to the main level for an immediate house meeting."

Grayson and his brothers looked at me a little weird and then Grayson let out a laugh.

"What's so funny?" I asked.

"Do you all seriously have an intercom system in the house?"

I shrugged. "Yeah, I mean … didn't you all?"

The three of them laughed and shook their heads. "No. No, we didn't. We just kind of texted each other if we needed something."

I hit Briar on his arm, "Whatever. Let's go before my dad has an aneurism because we're late."

We made our way to the main level, where two large tables were placed facing each other. My family was sitting at the table to my left and Camila stood between both tables. Camila's smile grew as we walked into the room.

Camila pointed at the empty table. "Welcome to the Light Fae's home. The Dark Royals may sit here as we come to some sort of agreement as to how long you all stay here and where we go from here."

I joined my family at their table and then noticed Grayson chose the chair that directly faced me from the other table.

We grinned at each other as the room got awkwardly silent.

My dad stood up. "Let me begin by saying how very sorry I am about the loss of your home. I can't imagine the anger and hurt you all are feeling right now."

Mr. Treble nodded, "Thank you, and we want to thank you for so quickly opening your doors to us, even though we are Dark Fae."

My mom smiled, "You all may be Dark, and us Light, but we all are Fae, and we all are facing the same danger—my sister and Sebastian."

Camila nodded in agreement. "We must set our past differences aside in order to beat Violet and Sebastian. It seems that they have a tremendous number of supporters. Does anyone here know what they're doing to entice these new followers of theirs?"

Everyone stayed quiet until Andre, the head Dark Royal guard, spoke. "I think the Fae are just being tempted by power and by the fact that Violet and Sebastian want to not only rule the Fae world, but the mundane world as well. I think they're being promised a lot."

Camila sighed, "There's no way they can believe that the humans will just allow some strange creatures to take over their world. My husband must have forgotten what happened in the 1690s."

We all stayed quiet. Camila went on, "The last time a group of Fae tried to take over the mundane world, our kind were accused of being witches and were hung and burned to death. And not only was it our kind, but a lot of innocent mundanes were murdered as well. It was a sad and dark time for everyone."

Camila's eyes looked as if they were suddenly filled with tears as she tried to remember the harsh past. "We lost so many. After the trials were over, we were all forced to go underground and into hiding again. Our neighborhoods were enchanted with Angel Oak Trees. The humans were unable to walk into our neighborhoods. The trees created somewhat of a black hole so the humans kind of just walked through our neighborhoods to their next destination."

"It must have been a sign then," I said.

"What was a sign?" Grayson asked.

"When they knocked down all of the Angel Oak trees and barricaded us in back at the hill side. At first, I thought they just did it because the trees would take forever for us to move, but it's the fact that they were Angel Oak trees. Violet knew what she was doing or saying, I guess."

Briar spoke now, "Yeah, I remember that. It was the first time we noticed that both Light and Dark Fae were working together."

Camila's eyes lit up as she suddenly remembered the events. "You both are correct. I don't know why I didn't think of it before. The slaying of Angel Oak trees is strictly frowned upon in our scriptures, because they offer us protection. They're basically a gift from our Gods. Sebastian and Violet probably uprooted those trees, not only to barricade you all, but also to get the chance at destroying something sacred."

"Anyone have any idea as to what their next move might be?" I asked.

Everyone stared blankly at each other for a few seconds.

"Well, if they attacked our home, it may be safe to assume that they're going to try and attack your home as well."

Hunter spoke up, "I assure you all, we are prepared for any sort of attack. There's no way they will get inside our gates."

Cayne quietly said, "That is what we thought. We thought all of our wards and gates were strong enough to protect us. I guess we were wrong."

My dad chimed in, "We have thoroughly interrogated all of our remaining guards. I feel confident in Hunter and his team."

Camila spoke now, "I don't think they're going to attack us here. They needed a place of their own. Somewhere my husband was familiar with ..."

Grayson finished Camila's sentence, "... that's why he chose our house. It's full of the darkness he needs, and he knows a lot of the Dark Fae guards still look up to him and his ways ..."

Mr. Treble began to shake his head, "You're right... and only he would know that our Dark Relics are there as well."

Mrs. Treble let out a small gasp, "He can't get his hands on those. He'll be able to do unimaginable things."

"What exactly could he do with them?" I asked.

Camila looked at the Trebles, and then at me. "He could possibly raise the dead."

CHAPTER FIFTY-TWO

"Raise the dead?" my dad shouted.

"That's beyond blasphemy!" my mom joined in.

Cayne spoke now, "That is why we, as the Dark Royal family, have control of them and have them hidden."

Briar added, "The Dark Relics do empower who ever has control of them, but as the Royal family, when we are of age, we are required to swear an oath of protection and not use them."

"If Sebastian gets the Relics and uses them, the world as we know is over," Mr. Treble said.

"Then we must attack now. We must combine the guards we have, and all of us attack them, to-night," my dad said.

Camila let out a long sigh, "I'm afraid there's no other option. We must strike while they don't expect us to. We can't give them the chance to settle in and find the Relics."

"Very well then. Let's do this," Mr. Treble said.

We all looked at each other and then my dad said, "Let's meet the guards in half an hour. Everyone, get what you need, quickly."

Everyone left the room and Grayson and I stayed behind.

He grabbed my hand and pulled me into his arms. "Are you ready for this?"

I embraced him and then looked up at him. "Am I ready to kick my aunt's ass? And get you your home back? Um, yeah."

He leaned down to kiss me and as our lips touched, that electricity ran through our bodies. Not only did I ignore it this time, he did as well.

"I need to go grab a few things and I'll meet you with the guards in a couple of minutes," Grayson said.

"Alright. I need to get with Alexia. I just want to make sure she's ready as well."

He nodded and we went our separate ways.

I headed up to Alexia's room and slowly walked in. She was sitting on her bed, with a bag of what looked like sand.

"Hey, I was just checking in on you. Are you ready for this?"

She squeezed the bag and nodded, "I'll be fine. I've got a secret weapon and I'm going to use it as soon as I can on Violet."

"Oh yeah, what is it?"

"You'll have to wait and see. Enough about me. Are you and your lover boy ready?" she teased.

"Yeah, I guess so. I mean, it's not like we have a choice."

She smiled, "Yeah, I guess you're right."

I reached for her hand. "Let's go kick some Dark Fae butt."

"They don't even know what's about to hit them, sis."

My sister and I walked downstairs and were surprised we were actually the first there, besides Hunter, of course.

"Hey there, tall man. You ready to get your hands a little dirty?" Alexia asked.

He laughed, "I was born for this. What about you, Miss?"

"Ew, don't call me Miss."

The three of us started laughing as the rest of the group joined us.

My dad spoke first, "Alright everyone, Hunter is going to cover the initial game plan."

We all looked back at Hunter, who cleared his throat before speaking.

"Alright, when we get to the Dark Royals' home, we are going to surround the house. Some of our guards are going to put up their blocking spells so we can go in, but they won't be able to come out. Once that is done, we're going to head straight in. The plan is for the Light Fae to distract the guards and Violet as the Dark Royals split up."

"Are you sure it's a good idea for us to split up?" Mrs. Treble asked.

"Yes. Some of you will be with Camila, looking for Sebastian, while the rest of you hunt down the Relics. We need you all to make sure they're safe."

Camila, who looked like a Goddess of War, spoke, "When we find Sebastian, I'm going to bind him."

"How do you know that you'll be able to?" Alexia asked.

Camila showed us a diamond-like item that was glowing with a golden light.

"This is from my home, Zion. He won't be able to break through it if I can get the binding done in time."

Hunter spoke again, "When we are there, we are not keeping survivors. The Light Fae who are there, are traitors and according to our laws, they must be killed as such."

We all nodded and then made our way out of our home.

The drive to the Dark Royals' home felt like forever. I could feel butterflies in my stomach, anxious and ready to be used for good.

I asked Alexia, "Did you bring that secret weapon sand of yours?"

She grinned as she held up a velvet bag. "You know I did. Violet's not going to know what hit her."

We finally made it to their home and saw that

our guards were already there, putting up the spell wards.

Alexia and I looked at each other, smiled, and got out of the car.

CHAPTER FIFTY-THREE

We began to walk towards the house and I felt the burning sensation run through my body. It was happening. My powers were coming through. I looked down and my skin was the familiar shades of purple and blue.

Grayson was by my side, smiling at me. "You're beautiful."

I felt my eyes burning their Elemancy Golden color and kissed his cheek. "I remember when this first happened to me. I was so scared. I was afraid. I didn't know what or who I was."

"And now?" he asked.

"And now, I know I was meant to take Sebastian and Violet down. That's why the Gods didn't force me to choose at my Reckoning. It was all for this."

"You're right. Hey, when this is all said and done, why don't we spend a week at our little old hidden place?"

"Sounds like a date."

We squeezed each other's hands and we noticed visible sparks coming from the two of us.

His eyes turned bright purple and we followed the guards inside of the home.

As soon as we entered the house, we were met by a large group of old Light Fae and Dark Fae.

A girl with orange hair headed towards me and began to throw fire balls at me.

"Is that all you've got?"

I smiled and felt a whip-like item in my hand that was glowing with a golden aura.

I struck my hand out and the whip grabbed the girl by her neck. I squeezed on it and pulled her close to me. She was so close that I could feel her panicked breath on my face.

"How dare you betray my family and the Light Fae. You are a disgrace."

I pulled on the whip and snapped her neck. As she fell to ground, I saw her eyes dim to a deep black.

I ran past her and noticed Camila heading upstairs with Mr. Treble and the twins.

Alexia was knocked down on the ground in front of the staircase. With my whip, I grabbed the Dark Fae who was fighting her.

As my whip wrapped around his legs, I felt a strong, painful electric current hit my back. I fell to the ground, not letting go of the Dark Fae until Alexia got up.

She shouted, "I've got it, sis. Take care of that bitch!"

I let go and turned around to see a small, petite blue-haired Light Fae smiling at me.

"Cheyenne? Is that you?"

The girl laughed, "You remember me? That makes this so much more fun."

She snapped her fingers and sent another electric current towards me. This time, it hit my shoulder.

I felt my body overheating with pain and anger. I used my left hand to call upon the wind, knocking Cheyenne off the table she was standing on.

I walked towards her and put my foot on her throat.

"Why? Why did you betray us?"

She spat out at me, "Your family is disgusting. If it

were up to you all, we'd be in hiding forever. What kind of life is that?"

I pushed down on her throat a little bit more. "That makes a safe life, that's what that makes, you idiot. Do you think the humans are going to just let Fae run around and live side-by-side with them?"

I lifted my foot a bit and she said, "Who said live side-by-side with humans? We're taking them out, too. This world is ours!"

As I pushed down on her throat again, she began to laugh.

"What's so funny?"

She put a blue pill in her mouth and her body began to convulse. A couple of seconds later, she was dead.

I ran around the house looking for Violet and saw Grayson fighting a couple of Dark Fae. He looked like he was in his element—like he was made for this. He was made for war.

He looked at me and grinned. I smiled back and continued to look for Violet.

Before I walked up another flight of stairs, I saw two Dark Fae holding my mom down. I ran to-wards them but right before I could reach either of them with my whip, they snapped my mom's neck.

I felt tears coming down my face. And although I felt a deep sadness, the first emotion was anger.

I screamed out, "Mom!" Her head slowly leaned towards me and I saw the bright blue light in them dim to the dark black of a dead Fae.

I ran closer to the two Fae who had killed her. I grabbed one with the whip and set the other on fire with a single finger snap.

The Dark Fae who was stuck in my whip was now on the ground and I sat on top of him. I pulled out a knife from my boot and looked into his purple eyes. I felt my eyes burning brighter than usual. I looked up and saw they were glowing a bright gold now.

I put the knife back into my boot and stared into the Dark Fae's eyes. I suddenly felt like I could control the intensity of my golden eyes. I turned them up to maximum and saw that I sent a burning light from my eyes into the Dark Fae's.

When I finally turned down the intensity, I saw that I burned his eyes straight through his body. There was nothing but blank holes where his eyes once were.

I looked up and saw Alexia. She was staring at me,

with nothing but blankness in her eyes.

She cried out, "Mom! No!"

She was shaking my mom's lifeless body.

I walked over to her and put my hand on her shoulder.

"Alexia, she's gone. We've got to move on."

My sister shrugged off my hand and was now silently crying, just tears coming down.

She slowly stood up and then faced me. "Let's find Violet and Sebastian. We are going to kill them."

My sister led the way up more stairs and her eyes were burning a beautiful blue.

We came across a hallway that split in two ways. "Let's split up here," I suggested.

"Alright. Be careful, Aria."

"You too. Go kick someone's ass."

She smiled at me as we walked down our different hallways.

CHAPTER FIFTY-FOUR

I headed down the hallway I had chosen and could hear fighting in almost every room. I made my way down the long corridor when I finally found a room with two guards outside of it.

"Hey! What are you doing here?" one of them shouted.

"Me? I'm looking for Violet. Tell me where she is, and I'll think about letting you live."

The guys looked at each other and then laughed.

Their eyes lit up the Dark Fae purple. The one with blue hair made a motion with his hands and suddenly, I felt like I was drowning. There was no water around me, but I felt as if he was holding my head in water.

He looked at his purple-haired friend and laughed, "This is too easy."

I felt my skin burning, hotter than ever before. I felt my eyes do the same. As I looked down, my entire body turned from the normal blues and shades of purple to a bright golden aura, similar to Camila's.

Suddenly, the drowning sensation was gone and I was able to catch my breath as I kneeled down.

I looked up and gave the two guards an evil grin.

The Fae who first attacked me tried again, and I held up my arm and saw a clear shield pop up.

"What's the matter? Your little magic trick not working anymore?"

His eyes were burning purple with frustration.

The Fae with the purple hair swirled his hands in a circular motion and sent a tornado-like figure towards me. I jumped up and ran across the sides of the walls in the hallway to dodge the strong force of wind.

I smiled again and busted out my new favorite toy, the golden whip.

I swung it at the blue-haired Fae and choked him until his eyes faded to black. Right before the purple-haired Fae could take the blue pill that Cheyenne had taken a while ago, I knocked his hand down with my whip and jumped up and landed on his shoulders. I lifted his head up towards me and kept pulling until I felt his neck snap.

Both Fae were now dead and I had to breathe for a second before I opened the door.

After a couple of seconds, I finally decided to open the door and walk inside.

The room looked a like high-end museum. I looked around in awe. The farther I travelled into the room, the stronger I felt a pulling sensation in my stomach.

I turned around as I heard someone a few steps behind me. I looked around and saw a door not too far from me. Without thinking, I ran into the room and slowly opened the door to peek out.

It was Mr. Treble, Mrs. Treble, Camila, and a few guards.

Camila's eyes were burning bright as she looked around the room.

"So this is it?" she asked.

"Yes, this is where we keep the Dark Relics," Mr. Treble responded.

"Exactly how many are there?"

Mrs. Treble answered now, "There are thirteen."

I was about to close the door to find another way out when one of the guards posted outside shouted, "Someone's in that room!!"

I opened the door with my hands up, above my head as if I were surrendering.

"Um, hi, sorry, it's just me …"

The group of Fae let out sighs of relief. Camila even almost laughed and then studied me.

"There's something different about you."

I felt a wave of emotion hit me like a ton of bricks.

"They killed my mom. Right in front of me."

And then it happened. My body was shaking as I cried and I could actually see my golden aura.

"I'm so very sorry about your mom," Camila said as she pulled me into her arms.

"Your mom was an amazing woman and she raised a courageous and blessed family," she continued.

"The Goddess has placed her hand upon you, Aria. I knew you had the power of Elemancy but this just proves it. She has approved of you."

I tried to speak through my tears, "Wha-what do you mean"?

"Your aura. It is nearly the same as mine. Long ago, shortly after Sebastian and I separated, the Goddess came to me in my dreams. She took me to Zion to help heal my heart. She has blessed us with powers unmatched. Consider me a sister, Aria."

I continued to cry as we heard chaos begin to happen from the other rooms.

"What is it?" Camila asked with a firm voice.

"It's the Relics," Mr. Treble said, worried, "Some of them are missing."

"What do you mean some of them are missing? Why would someone take a few of them and not all of them?"

After a minute or so, Mr. Treble looked around the room and then at us. "The Relics missing are those that can raise the dead."

"When I first walked into the room, I felt a weird pulling sensation in my stomach. I didn't know what it was. And then I heard you all and ran to hide in that room."

"The Relics were calling to you," Mrs. Treble said.

"When they feel a great power like their own, they'll call out to it." Camila said.

"Did you see anyone else here when you walked in?" Mrs. Treble asked.

I shook my head, "Nope. It was just the two morons that I took care of outside."

As I was talking I still felt warm tears falling down my face and an emptiness in my chest.

We were walking around the room making sure all the other Relics were still there when we heard a loud booming sound from down the hall.

We ran down the hall and I saw my dad, sister, and Grayson all fighting some Light Fae guards.

We ran towards them to help them out and as soon as we got there, more traitorous Light Fae appeared.

I pulled out my golden whip and knocked three of them down as Camila smiled at them, waved her hand, and snapped their necks in seconds.

"Whoa! Good one!" I told her.

"I'll teach you some time. It's quite easy. And your whip? That's an interesting choice of a weapon."

"Yeah, I don't know. It just feels right."

"Then follow the feeling," Camila said as she lifted her arms and threw a golden fireball at the rest of the Light Fae.

They went flying into the wall and we all fell down from the power of the attack.

As we stood up, we heard a male voice, "You fools! You come into our home and not only are you destroying it, but you have taken the remainder of our Relics? You will not get far!"

We looked around but didn't see anyone.

Camila's eyes were filled with fury.

"That, everyone, was Sebastian."

CHAPTER FIFTY-FIVE

We began to run around the hallway, looking through the different rooms for either Sebastian or Violet.

We kept running into their guards and dealing with them quite easily, but we had our eyes on the prize.

As we got back down to the main level of the house, Grayson suggested we go look in the lower part now.

As we all headed down to the lower level, we decided to break into two groups to make the search faster.

I was with Grayson, Alexia, Hunter, Cayne, and Mr. Treble.

We walked towards this long hallway that was pitch black.

"Okay, I've seen one too many scary movies. I know how us walking down this hallway is going to work," Alexia said quietly.

Grayson laughed as he brightened his deep purple eyes.

The rest of us followed suit, except my entire aura was on, lighting the entire room in my golden light's beauty.

As we got closer to a door at the end of the hallway, I could hear Sebastian's voice calling to me.

"Aria, your aunt told me how strong you were. I didn't believe her until tonight. Why don't you join us? We could do amazing things together."

I looked around and noticed I was the only one who could hear him.

"Get out of my head, asshole!"

He let out a devilish laugh, "Don't be a fool. If you don't join us, everyone you love will die."

Hunter and Grayson were on either side of me.

Grayson asked, "What's going on? Who are you talking to?"

"It's Sebastian. He's in my head. He wants me to join him and Violet."

"He must be close by," Mr. Treble said

We continued to walk towards the door, and when Grayson tried to open it, he was thrown back. He flew back about five feet and slowly stood back up.

"What the hell is that about?"

Hunter said, "It's been enchanted with Dark Relic magic."

"I'm sick of these Dark Relics. They can bring people back from the dead and enchant doors. Come on," Alexia said in frustration.

I walked closer to the door. "Let me try something."

I lifted my arms up and faced my palms towards the enchanted door.

My golden aura turned on, and as soon as I focused on the door, I could actually see the enchantment on it.

It was dark and swirled around the door like an oil-like substance.

I pushed my palms towards the door and golden arches slammed against the door and forced them open.

I pulled back my aura and smiled as everyone

looked at me in awe.

"What? I've learned a few things," I said.

We all entered the room cautiously and then as we turned a corner, we saw him. Sebastian.

He was sitting at the end of a long black table with a crown on his head.

"How dare you wear the Crown of Darkness!" Mr. Treble shouted.

Sebastian yawned and lifted his hand, and with a waving motion, threw Mr. Treble against the wall.

Grayson's eyes burned brightly as he began to run towards Sebastian.

I shouted, "Grayson! Stop!"

I was too late. Sebastian stopped Grayson in his tracks and tossed him against the same wall his dad had just hit, only this time the wall broke and Grayson flew into the next room.

I looked at Alexia, "Go check on Grayson and his dad, please. I've got this."

Then I turned to Hunter, "Go and get the others. I'll stall as long as I can."

Hunter looked at me hesitantly and then nodded, "I'll be right back. Be safe, Aria."

CHAPTER FIFTY-SIX

It was just me and him. I couldn't believe I was standing in front of Sebastian Harper. A few months ago, I would've been scared, but today I was just pissed off.

"Aria, are you here to join me and your aunt in our mission?"

"That's never going to happen. Speaking of my aunt, where is that bitch at?"

"Tsk, tsk, tsk. Don't use that language amongst royalty, Aria. You should know better."

I spit out at him in disgust.

I closed my eyes and let my body begin to burn with its intense, newfound power.

Sebastian stood up, surprise in his eyes.

"It's true. The Goddess has placed her hand upon you. You have the power of Elemancy. Oh, Aria. If you just joined us, the things we could do."

"You're sick. You actually believe that you can wipe out the human race?"

He smiled at me and said nothing.

He began to walk towards me and I felt a large, electric ball of energy in my palm. I let it grow until I couldn't stand the pain from the electricity anymore and then I threw it at him.

A bright blue and orange flaming ball went flying towards Sebastian as he jumped up in surprise.

He dusted off his shoulders. "Aw, darling, you missed me."

He rubbed his palms together and then a large orb filled with fire was coming right at me.

I did a backflip and barely dodged it. As I got back on my feet, Grayson ran in. "Are you alright?"

I nodded, "Are you alright?"

He smiled, "Camila healed my dad and me. They're going after Violet. They saw her outside."

"Ah, Grayson, you came to save your little damsel in distress?"

Grayson's eyes lit up with fury as mine grew their new bright golden color.

"She's no Damsel in distress. She can kick your ass any day. I'm just here to witness it."

Sebastian's eyes were bright, but they seemed to be glowing almost black now.

Sebastian began to run towards us when Grayson threw an electric current at him.

"Whoa, when did you learn how to do that?"

He smirked, "Do you think you're the only one who's learned new tricks?"

Sebastian stopped in his tracks and fell down on one knee.

I jumped up, did a flip, and landed behind him. I immediately took off the Relic Crown and tossed it across the room.

I used my golden whip to hold Sebastian in his place as he spat out at me, "Do you think this is it? Do you think you all are going to take me down this easily? You fools!"

Grayson walked towards us slowly as he showed off small electric currents from all of his fingertips.

"The great Sebastian Harper. The one who cannot be killed. The Original Dark Fae."

Grayson was now standing directly in front of Sebastian.

"How does it feel knowing that you're about to die? I'm going to make sure you feel every second of it. For my sister and for Aria's mom."

Sebastian laughed. "I welcome death like a dear friend. The real question is how do you all feel knowing your world is going to collapse whether I'm here to witness it or not?"

I squeezed my grip on the whip to choke Sebastian a little more.

Grayson looked at me and then said, "Aria, I've got an idea."

I looked up at him, "Oh yeah?"

He smiled, "Grab my hand. Let's end this."

Sebastian's eyes were glowing purple again, as if he were a normal Fae and not the Original Fae. He actually looked scared for once.

I smiled and grabbed onto my boyfriend's hand. As soon as we touched, we channeled our destructive fire into my whip.

The second I felt the electricity in my hand, I pulled on the whip and snapped Sebastian's head right off.

I took a step back as his body collapsed and black blood spewed out everywhere.

Grayson smiled and ran to the Relic Crown.

"I knew that destructive fire would not end us," Grayson said.

He leaned in and kissed me, his electric current filling my body with excitement and happiness.

"It didn't end us, but it ended someone," I laughed.

"Should we go find the others? They were going outside to find Violet," Grayson said.

I nodded and we left Sebastian's lifeless body on the floor.

CHAPTER FIFTY-SEVEN

Grayson and I headed outside and as we heard my dad and Alexia crying, I knew where they were.

We ran around a couple of corners and found everyone standing in a circle.

Suddenly the tsunami of sadness hit me again. My mom was dead. Camila was rubbing my shoulders as she spoke. "Adalyn was a brave and strong woman. She raised an incredible family and I know she's with our Goddess watching over us all now. We must not forget why we came here tonight. We must find Violet and Sebastian—"

Grayson cut her off, "Sebastian is dead."

Everyone let out what sounded like a gasp.

"Aria and I took care of him with some of our little new magic tricks," he smirked.

"I thought you all were chasing Violet?" I asked

through my tears.

"We were, she had a getaway car waiting for her. The rest of their guards left as well."

"Well, I did manage to get the Relic Crown from Sebastian," Grayson added.

"That's great, although I'm still afraid that Violet has the Relics needed for necromancy," Camila responded.

Hunter, Andre, and a few other guards pulled up in a long SUV, parked, and then slowly walked towards us.

"Mr. Whitelace, would you like us to take her home?" Hunter asked, looking at my mother.

My dad, crying and holding Alexia, nodded, "Ye-yes. Thank you, Hunter."

Hunter nodded and then whispered, "I am so very sorry for all of your loss. Mrs. Whitelace was an amazing leader and Fae."

He signaled for Andre and the other Fae to join him and they took my mom's body and loaded her into the SUV.

When they drove off, Camila broke the silence.

"Before we head back to your home, Mr. Whitelace, may I suggest that we all search the ground to ensure no one was left behind? We also need to get the remainder of the Dark Relics moved."

My dad nodded as Mr. Treble spoke now, "The Dark Relics have already been taken to a secret safe house. Only our family and Andre know its location."

"Very well then," Camila said.

We all walked back into the house and started to look around for anyone who may have been able to tell us where Violet was going.

Alexia was too torn up about my mom, so she left with my dad.

Grayson, his brothers, and I were walking together as we headed to the kitchen. When we walked in, all of us looked at each other and then at the heads on the wall.

There was a line of Light Fae heads mounted on the wall. And above them, in blood, Violet had left us a note:

My sister is dead. I am not. The strongest survived, and now, your world shall rot.

My cell phone rang. It was an unknown number. I picked it up and my entire body went ice-cold.

"Hello, cousin. Have you missed me? ... Hello?

Aria? It's me, your favorite cousin Ethan. I'll see you soon."

I hung up the phone and looked up at the guys.

"Violet has already brought someone back from the dead."

"What? Who?" Grayson asked.

"My cousin Ethan is alive."

THE END

YOU CAN FIND MORE FROM ABEL:

Website: http://abelozuna.com

Books: http://buyabelobooks.com

Instagram: http://instagram.com/abelozuna4

Podcast Network: http://creativecentralnetwork.com

Facebook: http://facebook.com/abelozuna04

ABOUT THE AUTHOR

Abel Ozuna

 Abel Ozuna was born and raised in Corpus Christi, TX. Not only is Abel a published author, but he is also owner of the Creative Central Network - a home for podcasters and creatives.

When Abel is not podcasting, writing, or working on social media, he enjoys spending time with his family, close friends, reading, and listening to podcasts (especially murder mystery podcasts!)